Samuel French Acting Edition

I0591858

Leader Of The Pack: The Ellie Greenwich Musical

Book by
Anne Beatts

Music and Lyrics by
Ellie Greenwich & Friends

Based on the original play by
Melanie Mintz

Additional Material by
Jack Heifner

FOR PRODUCTION INQUIRIES

UNITED STATES AND CANADA
info@concordtheatricals.com
1-866-979-0447

UNITED KINGDOM AND EUROPE
licensing@concordtheatricals.co.uk
020-7054-7200

Each title is subject to availability from Concord Theatricals Corp.,
depending upon country of performance. Please be aware that *LEADER
OF THE PACK: THE ELLIE GREENWICH MUSICAL* may not be
licensed by Concord Theatricals Corp. in your territory. Professional
and amateur producers should contact the nearest Concord Theatricals
Corp. office or licensing partner to verify availability.

This work is published by Samuel French, an imprint of Concord Theatricals Corp.

For all inquiries regarding motion picture, television, online/digital and other media rights, please contact Concord Theatricals Corp.

MUSIC AND THIRD-PARTY MATERIALS USE NOTE

Licensees are solely responsible for obtaining formal written permission from copyright owners to use copyrighted music and/or other copyrighted third-party materials (e.g., artworks, logos) in the performance of this play and are strongly cautioned to do so. If no such permission is obtained by the licensee, then the licensee must use only original music and materials that the licensee owns and controls. Licensees are solely responsible and liable for clearances of all third-party copyrighted materials, including without limitation music, and shall indemnify the copyright owners of the play(s) and their licensing agent, Concord Theatricals Corp., against any costs, expenses, losses and liabilities arising from the use of such copyrighted third-party materials by licensees. For music, please contact the appropriate music licensing authority in your territory for the rights to any incidental music.

IMPORTANT BILLING AND CREDIT REQUIREMENTS

If you have obtained performance rights to this title, please refer to your licensing agreement for important billing and credit requirements.

LEADER OF THE PACK premiered at the Ambassador Theatre in New York on April 8, 1985. The performance was directed and choreographed by Michael Peters, with sets by Tony Walton, costumes by Robert de Mora, and lighting design by Pamela Cooper. The cast was as follows:

DARLENE LOVE	Darlene Love
ANNIE GOLDEN	Annie Golden
YOUNG ELLIE GREENWICH (1960s)	Dinah Manoff
ROSIE	Zora Rasmussen
SHELLEY	Barbara Yeager
MICKEY	Jasmine Guy
JEFF BARRY	Patrick Cassidy
GUS SHARKEY	Dennis Bailey
DISK JOCKEY VOICE	Peter Neptune
WAITRESS	Jasmine Guy
LOUNGE SINGER	Pattie Darcy
DANCE COUPLE	Shirley Black-Brown & Keith McDaniel
GINA	Gina Taylor
ELLIE GREENWICH (1980s)	Ellie Greenwich

CHARACTERS

DARLENE LOVE

ANNIE GOLDEN

YOUNG ELLIE GREENWICH (1960S)

ROSIE

SHELLEY

MICKEY

JEFF BARRY

GUS SHARKEY

DISK JOCKEY VOICE

WAITRESS

LOUNGE SINGER

DANCE COUPLE

*ELLIE GREENWICH (1980S)

SETTING

The action takes place here and now and in the days of beehives and 45s.

ACKNOWLEDGEMENTS

Ellie Greenwich wishes to acknowledge the following persons who have had a significant impact on her career. First and foremost is her former husband, Jeff Barry, a truly gifted musical talent, who made writing easy and fun. Super songwriters Jerry Leiber and Mike Stoeller, the brilliant Phil Spector, George "Shadow" Morton, Tony Powers, Desmond Child, Steve Tudanger, and Jeff Kent. To talented singers like Tina Turner, Lesley Gore, The Ronettes, Irene Cara, Neil Diamond, Nona Hendryx, Cyndi Lauper, and Ellen Foley. Ellie thanks you for performing her songs with such excellence. The acknowledgement of performers cannot be complete without a special thanks to Darlene Love, whose talent made many of the songs the hits they were. Ellie deeply thanks her friends for being there, and a very special thanks and expression of love to her sister Laura, for more things than can be mentioned. Finally, she wants to dedicate this show to her late parents, William and Rose Greenwich. I miss you.

---

*ELLIE and YOUNG ELLIE may be the same performer, or ELLIE may be played by the actress who plays ROSIE earlier in the show (In the Broadway production, ELLIE was the real Ellie Greenwich).

ACT I

ACT II

[MUSIC NO. 01 "OPENING"]

(Dance Opening.)

[MUSIC NO. 01A "OPENING – DANCE"]

(The show curtain, which resembles a large phonograph record, rises to reveal the set: a series of giant record platters. No one is onstage.)

*(Four **CHORUS BOYS** enter, one at a time, dressed in contemporary [1980s] costume. Each does a "specialty" dance indicative of "present day," according to each **BOY**'s individual talents: one might do a breakdance, another perhaps a somersault. Then they dance together.)*

*(Four **CHORUS GIRLS** enter, also in contemporary costume. The **BOYS** flirt with the **GIRLS**, and the **BOYS** exit, waving. The **GIRLS** now do a dance of their own.)*

*(Finally, the **BOYS** re-enter, and the whole **COMPANY** dances to a big finish. All freeze.)*

*(**DARLENE** enters stage left.)*

[MUSIC NO. 01B "AFTER OPENING"]

DARLENE. Now that's eighties – *(Drum accent. The **COMPANY** shift positions and "freeze" again.)* – but hold onto that for awhile. We'll come back to it later. Right now we're going to take a trip back to the sixties.

> *(Drum accent. The **COMPANY** again shift positions and "re-freeze.")*

[MUSIC NO. 02 "BE MY BABY"]

If you were around in 1963 – wherever you were, whatever you were doing – the radio was playing this song...

*(ANNIE, **JASMINE**, and **BARBARA** enter in exaggerated 1960s costumes, with giant beehive hairdos. In the Broadway production, these hairdos flew off during the following number to reveal normal-sized beehive wigs.)*

ANNIE.

THE NIGHT WE MET I KNEW
   I NEEDED YOU SO
AND IF I HAD THE CHANCE
   I'D NEVER LET YOU GO   **LADIES.**
SO WON'T YOU SAY YOU   OOOO…
   LOVE ME
I'LL MAKE YOU SO PROUD   OOOO…
   OF ME
WE'LL MAKE THEM TURN   OOOO…
   THEIR HEADS
EVERY PLACE WE GO.   OOOO…

SO WON'T YOU PLEASE

LADIES.

BE MY, BE MY BABY

ANNIE.

BE MY LITTLE BABY…

LADIES.

MY ONE AND ONLY BABY

ANNIE.

SAY YOU'LL BE MY DARLIN'…

LADIES.

…BE MY, BE MY BABY

ANNIE.

BE MY BABY NOW…

LADIES.

MY ONE AND ONLY BABY

ANNIE.

WO… WO… WO… WO…

    (Instrumental.)

ANNIE.	LADIES.
I'LL MAKE YOU HAPPY BABY	OOOO…
JUST WAIT AND SEE	OOOO…
FOR EVERY KISS YOU GIVE ME	OOOO…
I'LL GIVE YOU THREE	OOOO…
OH, SINCE THE DAY I SAW YOU	AH…
I HAVE BEEN WAITING FOR YOU	AH…
YOU KNOW I WILL ADORE YOU	AH…
'TIL ETERNITY	AH…

SO WON'T YOU PLEASE

LADIES.

BE MY, BE MY BABY

ANNIE.

BE MY LITTLE BABY…

LADIES.

MY ONE AND ONLY BABY

ANNIE.

SAY YOU'LL BE MY DARLIN'…

LADIES.

…BE MY, BE MY BABY

ANNIE.

BE MY BABY NOW…

LADIES.

MY ONE AND ONLY BABY

ANNIE.

WO… WO… WO… WO…

LADIES.

OOOO…

ANNIE.

SO COME ON AND PLEASE

LADIES.

BE MY, BE MY BABY

ANNIE.

BE MY LITTLE BABY...

LADIES.

MY ONE AND ONLY BABY

ANNIE.

SAY YOU'LL BE MY DARLIN'...

LADIES.

...BE MY, BE MY BABY

ANNIE.

BE MY BABY NOW

LADIES.

MY ONE AND ONLY BABY

ANNIE.

WO... WO... WO... WO...

LADIES.

BE MY, BE MY BABY

ANNIE.

OOOO...

LADIES.

MY ONE AND ONLY BABY

ANNIE.

OOOO...

LADIES.

BE MY, BE MY BABY

ANNIE.

OOOO...

LADIES.

MY ONE AND ONLY BABY

ANNIE.

UH WO OH OH OH OH...

(**ANNIE, JASMINE,** *and* **BARBARA** *exit as* **DARLENE** *re-enters.*)

[MUSIC NO. 02A "BE MY BABY – CROSSOVER"]

DARLENE. Now I'm going to take you on a musical journey through the record kingdom and tell you about a girl whose songs sold a phenomenal one hundred million records. Why do I get to tell you this story? Because I'm Darlene Love and, babies, I was there.

[MUSIC NO. 03 "WAIT 'TIL MY BOBBY GETS HOME"]

(The entire **ENSEMBLE** *enters.)*

(They sing back-up and dance behind **DARLENE***'s solo.)*

YOU'VE BEEN CALLIN' ON ME EVERY DAY
EVER SINCE MY BOBBY WENT AWAY
YOU'VE BEEN KNOCKIN' ON MY FRONT DOOR
AND I KNOW JUST WHAT YOU'RE LOOKIN' FOR...
BUT
EVEN THOUGH YOU REALLY LOOK SO FINE
AND WE COULD HAVE A GOOD TIME

I'M GONNA

ALL.

WAIT 'TIL MY BOBBY GETS HOME
WAIT 'TIL MY BABY GETS HOME

DARLENE.

YEAH, YEAH, YEAH YOU BETTER LEAVE ME ALONE

ALL.

SURE I NEED SOME LOVIN' AND A-KISSIN' AND A-HUGGIN'
BUT I'LL WAIT 'TIL MY BOBBY GETS HOME

DARLENE.

YOU WANNA TAKE ME TO A MOVIE SHOW
I GOTTA TELL YOU THAT I JUST CAN'T GO
I KNOW MY BOBBY'S GONNA CALL TONIGHT
I WANNA TELL HIM EVERYTHING'S ALL RIGHT...
SO
THOUGH I HAVEN'T GOT A THING TO DO (AND I)
I'M SO LONELY AND BLUE

I'M GONNA...

ALL.

WAIT 'TIL MY BOBBY GETS HOME

WAIT 'TIL MY BABY GETS HOME

DARLENE.

YEAH, YEAH, YEAH YOU BETTER LEAVE ME ALONE

ALL.

SURE I NEED SOME LOVIN' AND A-KISSIN' AND A-HUGGIN'
BUT I'LL WAIT 'TIL MY BOBBY GETS HOME.

(Instrumental – Dance Break.)

OOO...

DARLENE.

I'M GONNA WAIT...

ALL.

WAIT 'TIL MY BOBBY GETS HOME
WAIT 'TIL MY BABY GETS HOME

DARLENE.

YEAH, YEAH, YEAH YOU BETTER LEAVE ME ALONE

ALL.

SURE I NEED SOME LOVIN' AND A-KISSIN' AND A-HUGGIN'
BUT I'LL WAIT 'TIL MY BOBBY GETS HOME

DARLENE.

OH...

ALL.

WAIT 'TIL MY BOBBY GETS HOME

DARLENE.

I'M GONNA WAIT...

ALL.

WAIT 'TIL MY BOBBY GETS HOME

DARLENE.

WAIT, WAIT...

ALL.

WAIT 'TIL MY BOBBY GETS HOME.

[MUSIC NO. 03A "WAIT 'TIL MY BOBBY – CROSSOVER"]

DARLENE. Now let's go back to where it all started. (*Moves right with the* **ENSEMBLE**.) Once upon a time a girl was born in a house at the corner of Starlight and Springtime Lanes... I'm not making this up. And this girl started writing songs on an accordion…really she did.

[MUSIC NO. 04 "A… MY NAME IS ELLIE"]

(**DARLENE** *exits.*)

(*Lights come up on* **YOUNG ELLIE** *singing and playing the accordion as the scene changes. In the Broadway production, the center circular platform, resembling a giant phonograph record, revolved to bring* **YOUNG ELLIE** *into place.*)

ELLIE.

A… MY NAME IS ELLIE
AND MY MAMA'S NAME IS MUSIC
I COME FROM A PLACE CALLED LEVITTOWN
WHERE I SANG MY SONGS
AND MY MAMA HELPED ME WRITE 'EM DOWN.

A… MY NAME IS ELLIE
AND I CALLED MY DADDY DADDY
THEY TOLD ME SKIES THEY WERE ALWAYS BLUE
FUNNY HOW MY MAMA AND DADDY ALWAYS KNEW.

(**ROSIE**, *her mother, enters left, and goes center. She kneels and starts pinning up* **ELLIE***'s skirt, taking the pins from a pincushion on her wrist.*)

(**ELLIE** *continues to practice, a cappella.*)

SHORT SKIRTS
UM BALOTTA, UM BALOTTA
HOW I LOVE TO SEE MY BABY'S KNEES.

(**ROSIE** *sticks* **ELLIE** *with a pin.*) Ow!

ROSIE. Hold still, Eleanor.

ELLIE. Ma, I'm practicing. Don't you want me to sound good for the Hadassah ladies?

ROSIE. (*Rises and takes accordion from* **ELLIE***'s shoulders.*) Eleanor, you gotta stop pushing yourself with the work, work, work!

ELLIE. But Ma…didn't you ever want something so bad you couldn't think about anything else?

ROSIE. Sure. I wanted to marry your father, have a family, and move out of Brooklyn to someplace exciting, like Levittown.

ELLIE. Yeah...well I want to fall in love someday, but more than anything I want to hear my songs played on the radio.

ROSIE. They'll be playing them.

ELLIE. You think so?

ROSIE. I know two things for sure. One, you're going to become the most famous songwriter in the entire world...

ELLIE. That's nice, Ma.

ROSIE. And two – when that doesn't work out, you're going to get a teaching degree to fall back on.

ELLIE. Ma!

> (SHELLEY, *in a matching Jivette costume, enters right and runs center.* ROSIE, *carrying* ELLIE*'s accordion, exits right.*)

SHELLEY. *(Calling.)* Ellie! *(Seeing* ROSIE.*)* Hiya, Mrs. Greenwich! Hey, Ellie! You look boss!

ELLIE. Yeah? You, too!

SHELLEY. Listen, I ran into this guy at the Burgerama who, get this, knows a guy who works in the Brill Building in the city, and get this – this guy says if this guy who this guy he knows knows, really digs your songs, we could make ourselves a record!

ELLIE. Shelley! You mean it? This guy really knows this guy who knows this guy? Oh, wow! This could be the Jivettes' big break! I'd die if we got on American Bandstand! Just die!

> (*The third Jivette,* MICKEY, *enters left, wearing her matching outfit.*)

SHELLEY. Hey, Mickey, have you heard the latest?

MICKEY. Yeah, Elvis was drafted. I'm gonna kill myself.

ELLIE. *(Leading the* **JIVETTES** *downstage onto the stage floor.)* Well, wait a few days, 'cause we've got a chance to go into the city and record the Jivette Boogie Beat!

[MUSIC NO. 05 "JIVETTE BOOGIE BEAT"]

(All three **JIVETTES** *jump up and down and scream. They go into the Jivette cheer.)*

ELLIE, SHELLEY, MICKEY.

WE DON'T SMOKE AND WE DON'T PET
BUT WE'RE THE HIPPEST YOU CAN GET
WE'RE NOT JIVE, WE'RE JUST – JIVETTES!

ELLIE.

BOOGIE!

SHELLEY.

OOGIE!

MICKEY.

WOOGIE!

ELLIE, SHELLEY, MICKEY.

BOO!
JIVETTES! JIVETTES! OO, OO, OO!
JIVETTE BOOGIE
LISTEN TO THE JIVETTE BOOGIE

ELLIE.

NOW THERE ARE MANY BOOGIES UP TO DATE
BUT HERE'S THE BOOGIE THAT'S REALLY GREAT

ELLIE, SHELLEY, MICKEY.

THE JIVETTE BOOGIE'S GOT THE BOOGIEST, WOOGIEST
    BEAT
THE JIVETTE BOOGIE IS SOLID AND CONCRETE
YOU GRAB YOUR BABY AND SWING HER OFF HER FEET

DO IT HIGH – DO IT LOW
DO IT FAST – DO IT SLOW

YOU GRAB YOUR BABY AND DO-SI-DO
SWING HER 'ROUND, TO AND FRO...

TO THAT JIVETTE BOOGIE BEAT...

(JIVETTE, JIVETTE BOOGIE BEAT)
JIVETTE, JIVETTE BOOGIE BEAT
JIVETTE, JIVETTE BOOGIE BEAT

[MUSIC NO. 05A "WRITERS' CROSSOVER"]

(The Brill Building.)

*(**JEFF**, wearing dark glasses and carrying a sheet of music, enters right and crosses left.)*

*(**KEITH**, wearing dark glasses, enters left and goes right.)*

JEFF.

KEITH, MY MAN!

KEITH.

HEY, JEFF, WHAT'S HAPPENING, BABY?

*(He crosses right, downstage of **JEFF**.)*

*(**PETER**, wearing dark glasses, enters left and crosses right to **JEFF**.)*

JEFF.

PETE!

PETER.

YEAH, MAN, HIP ME TO THE HAPS.

*(He crosses right, downstage of **JEFF**.)*

*(**LON**, wearing dark glasses, enters left and goes to **JEFF**'s left.)*

LON.

HI YA, J.B., WHAT'S THE GOOD WORD?

*(**ELLIE** enters right, and goes left under the platters to the upright piano, which moves onstage.)*

*(**JOEY**, wearing dark glasses, enters left and goes to **LON**'s left.)*

JOEY.

HEY, JEFF...

JEFF.

YEAH?

*(**KEITH**, **PETER**, **LON**, and **JOEY** walk off right, downstage of **JEFF**, in rhythm.)*

JOEY. *(As he passes **JEFF**.)*
DIG YOUR NEW TUNE!

(Inside the Brill Building.)

*(**ELLIE** is at the piano, picking out "Why Do Lovers Break Each Other's Hearts" when **JEFF**, following the writers right, stops and goes up to her back.)*

JEFF. Well, hello there.

ELLIE. *(Startled, she turns around, swings into action.)* Now you're going to listen to me, Mr. Sharkey...

JEFF. *(Backing off while interrupting.)* Wait a minute! Calm down! I'm not Gus Sharkey, the big producer.

ELLIE. *(Calming down.)* You're not?

JEFF. No – I'm just a writer here.

ELLIE. Oh, yeah? What do you write?

JEFF. Hit songs.

ELLIE. Oh, really? Well, I'm here trying to get a job.

JEFF. "Get a Job." The Silhouettes, 1958.

ELLIE. "Silhouettes." The Rays, 1957.

JEFF. *(Backing left.)* Hey, very good. Very good. Hope to see you around.

ELLIE. I certainly hope so.

*(**JEFF** exits left.)*

*(**ELLIE** returns to the piano and sings while playing her song.)*

GUS. *(Entering up left, hearing her play, jumps on top of piano.)* Who are you?

ELLIE. *(Making sure before she proceeds.)* Ellie Greenwich. Who are you?

GUS. Gus Sharkey.

ELLIE. *(She attacks.)* Uh-huh! *(**GUS** falls off the piano.)* Now you're going to listen to me, Mr. Sharkey! I sent you a song a couple of years ago that the Jivettes had hoped to record.

GUS. *(Not understanding, he interrupts.)* The Jivettes?

ELLIE. Yes and you returned it. So since my parents made me finish school, it's taken me all this time to get around to accepting your offer.

GUS. What offer?

ELLIE. Your letter said, and I quote "The Jivette Boogie Beat is the silliest, most out-of-date song I've ever heard, and if you ever write anything else feel free to come play it for me because I can always use a good laugh." So here I am and you can start laughing now.

> *(She plays and sings a few lines from "Why Do Lovers Break Each Other's Hearts".)*
>
> *(She stops and looks at GUS.)*

GUS. I love it!

ELLIE. You love it?

GUS. It's a hit!

ELLIE. It is good, isn't it?

GUS. *(Tries to grab the music from the piano.)* I've got to have it!

ELLIE. *(Stopping him.)* Now, now, Mr. Sharkey, you can't just have it! I'm no fool. The only way you'll get this song is to give me a job writing here.

GUS. All right, but I can't pay you a penny more than seventy-five dollars a week.

ELLIE. Make it one hundred.

GUS. All right, one hundred, but I get publishing rights.

ELLIE. All right, publishing rights, but I get two…coffee breaks.

GUS. All right. It's a deal. *(They shake hands.)*

ELLIE. You see, I drive a very hard bargain, Mr. Sharkey.

GUS. A very hard bargain indeed, Miss Greenwich. Now get to work.

(He closes lid over piano keys, then sits on lid with his leg stretched out the length of the piano.)

I think the intro ought to go something like this...

[MUSIC NO. 06 "WHY DO LOVERS BREAK EACH OTHER'S HEARTS"]

GUS & MEN. *(Repeat until* **DARLENE** *is in place.)*

DOOM BAH BAH DOOM BAH BAH
DOOM BAH BAH DOOM BAH BAH
DOOM BAH BAH DOOM BAH BAH
DOOM BAH BAH DOOM BAH BAH
DOOM BAH BAH DOOM BAH BAH
DOOM BAH BAH DOOM BAH BAH
DOOM BAH BAH DOOM BAH BAH
DOOM BAH BAH DOOM BAH BAH

*(***DARLENE** *and* **BACK-UP SINGERS** *enter through a giant radio set.)*

DARLENE.

DARLENE	ALL
WHY DO LOVERS	
BREAK EACH OTHER'S	
HEARTS?	
OH, TELL ME WHY DO	
LOVERS	
HAVE TO DRIFT APART?	**ALL.**
WHEN WE MET THE	OOO...
WORLD WAS BRIGHT	
NOW I'M CRYIN' EVERY	OOO... WAH...
NIGHT	
WHY DO LOVERS	OOO...
BREAK EACH OTHER'S	OOO...
HEARTS?	

ALL.

SHU DO BE DO, SHU DO BE DO
SHU DO BE DO, BE DO WAH

DARLENE.	ALL.
WHY DO LOVERS	OOO...

BREAK EACH OTHER'S HEARTS?	OOO…
OH, TELL ME WHY CAN'T LOVERS	OOO…
FINISH WHAT THEY START?	OOO… WAH…
A YEAR AGO WE WERE ONE,	OOO…
NOW JUST LOOK AT WHAT WE'VE DONE	OOO… WAH…
WHY DO LOVERS	OOO…
BREAK EACH OTHER'S HEARTS?	OOO…

ALL.

SHU DO BE DO, SHU DO BE DO
SHU DO BE DO, BE DO WAH

DARLENE.	**ALL.**
HELP ME, HELP ME,	AH…
I DON'T UNDERSTAND	
WHY WE ALWAYS	AH…
HURT THE ONE WE LOVE	
TELL ME, TELL ME,	AH…
WHERE'S THE LIFE WE PLANNED?	
WHERE ARE THE DREAMS THAT	WHOP WHOP
WE WERE DREAMIN' OF…?	WHOP WHOP
	WHOP WHOP
	WHOP WHOP
	WHOP WHOP
WHY DO LOVERS	OOO…
BREAK EACH OTHER'S HEARTS?	OOO… WAH…
OH, TELL ME WHY CAN'T LOVERS	OOO…
FINISH WHAT THEY START?	OOO… WAH…
A YEAR AGO WE WERE ONE,	OOO…
NOW JUST LOOK AT WHAT WE'VE DONE	OOO… WAH…
WHY DO LOVERS	OOO…

BREAK EACH OTHER'S HEARTS?	OOO...

ALL.

SHU DO BE DO, SHU DO BE DO
SHU DO BE DO, BE DO WAH

(Dance break.)

DARLENE.	**ALL.**
A YEAR AGO WE WERE ONE,	OOO... WAH...
NOW JUST LOOK AT WHAT WE'VE DONE	OOO... WAH...
WHY DO LOVERS	OOO...
BREAK EACH OTHER'S HEARTS?	

ALL. *(With* **DARLENE** *riffing.)*

WHY DO LOVERS
BREAK EACH OTHER'S HEARTS?
WHY DO LOVERS
BREAK EACH OTHER'S HEARTS?
WHY DO LOVERS
BREAK EACH OTHER'S HEARTS?

SHU DO BE DO, SHU DO BE DO
SHU DO BE DO, BE DO WAH

(Blackout. The **COMPANY** *exits.)*

[MUSIC NO. 06A "AFTER – WHY DO LOVERS..."]

(Lights up on **ELLIE**, *down left, wearing the accordion. She is looking at the back of her legs to make certain her seams are straight.)*

ELLIE.

BOMP SHU BOM...

*(***JEFF** *enters down right, sees* **ELLIE**, *puts on dark glasses he has taken from his pocket, goes left, leans against a "platter" platform, and harmonizes with her.)*

JEFF & ELLIE.

BOMP SHU BOM SHU BOMP...

*(**ELLIE** notices **JEFF**.)*

JEFF. That's perfect harmony.

ELLIE. Yeah?

JEFF. *(Goes left to **ELLIE**.)* You look real familiar.

ELLIE.

YOU DON'T REMEMBER ME, BUT I REMEMBER YOU.

JEFF. "Tears on My Pillow." 1958.

ELLIE. Little Anthony and the Imperials. We ran into each other downstairs in Gus' office about a year ago.

JEFF. Oh, yeah...so do you always play at office parties?

ELLIE. *(She escapes from his advances by going right, downstage of him.)* Sure. Every time Gus breaks the top ten, I break out the old accordion. *(Away from him.)* So – are you still writing hit songs?

JEFF. Sure. Ever hear of "Tell Laura I Love Her?"

ELLIE. Jeff Barry.

JEFF. That's me.

ELLIE. Oh, yeah? *(Turns right.)* Well, have you ever heard of a little number called "Why Do Lovers Break Each Other's Hearts?"

JEFF. That's Ellie Greenwich.

ELLIE. *(Faces **JEFF**.)* Ta da!

JEFF. That's you?

ELLIE. Live and in person!

JEFF. Well, well... *(He takes off dark glasses.)* What kind of music do you like?

ELLIE. Besides yours and mine?

JEFF. Besides ours.

ELLIE. *(Backs right, **JEFF** follows.)* Well, the Shirelles really send me – "Will You Still Love Me Tomorrow?"

JEFF. Like "Tonight's The Night," right? How about "Have You Ever Been Lonely?"

ELLIE. Yes, I'm "Lonesome Tonight."

JEFF. "I Gotta Know..."

ELLIE. *(Cutting him off.)* Elvis.

JEFF. "I'm All Shook Up." "Is There Any Chance."

ELLIE. *(She runs away from* **JEFF** *by going left, downstage of him. He follows.)* "A Million To One."

JEFF. "Don't Be Cruel."

ELLIE. *(As far left as she can go.)* "I'm Sorry." Brenda Lee.

JEFF. *(Very close to her.)* "If I Can't Have You…"

ELLIE. *(Cutting him off again.)* Etta James and Harvey.

JEFF. *(Amazed; goes closer to her.)* You know that? Then I gotta have you –

ELLIE. "No."

ELLIE & JEFF. By Dodie Stevens.

> *(***ELLIE** *turns and runs right.)*

JEFF. *(Trying to stop her.)* Wait, come back, stay.

ELLIE. *(Stops and turns toward him.)* "Stay" by Maurice Williams and the Zodiacs, right?

JEFF. Right.

> ### *[MUSIC NO. 07 "TODAY I MET THE BOY I'M GOING TO MARRY"]*
>
> *(***JEFF** *and* **ELLIE** *begin to exit as* **DARLENE** *and the* **COMPANY** *enter stage right. All are now in 1960s dress. During the following number, the* **ENSEMBLE** *couples off and dances as if at a prom.)*

TODAY I MET THE BOY I'M GONNA MARRY

OFFSTAGE VOICES. AHHH… *(Continues under the following vocal.)*

DARLENE.

TODAY I MET THE BOY I'M GONNA MARRY

> *(***JEFF** *exits left.)*

HE'S JUST WHAT I'VE BEEN WAITING FOR –
OH YEAH –
HE SMILED AT ME AND GEE THE MUSIC STARTED PLAYIN'

> *(***ELLIE** *exits right.)*

HERE COMES THE BRIDE WHEN HE WALKED
THROUGH THE DOOR

TODAY I MET THE BOY I'M GONNA MARRY
THE BOY WHOSE LIFE AND DREAMS AND LOVE I WANNA
    SHARE
FOR ON MY HAND A BAND OF GOLD APPEARED BEFORE ME
THE BAND OF GOLD I ALWAYS DREAMED I'D WEAR

WHEN WE KISSED...
I FELT A SWEET SENSATION
THIS TIME IT WASN'T JUST MY
IMAGINATION

TODAY I MET THE BOY I'M GONNA MARRY
HE'S JUST WHAT I'VE BEEN WAITING FOR...
OH, YEAH
WITH EVERY KISS OH THIS IS IT, MY HEART KEEPS SAYIN'
TODAY I MET THE BOY

WHEN WE KISSED...
I FELT A SWEET SENSATION
THIS TIME IT WASN'T MY
IMAGINATION

TODAY I MET THE BOY I'M GONNA MARRY
HE'S JUST WHAT I'VE BEEN WAITING FOR...
OH, YEAH WITH EVERY KISS OH THIS IS IT MY HEART KEEPS
    SAYIN'
TODAY I MET THE BOY I'M GONNA MARRY

    (**ELLIE** *enters right.*)

YEAH, YEAH, YEAH
OH YEAH,
TODAY I MET... I MET THE BOY...
THE BOY I'M GONNA MARRY.

    (**DARLENE**, *having made her way across the stage
    during the song, exits stage left.*)

    ***[MUSIC NO. 07A "TODAY I MET THE BOY –
    CROSSOVER"]***

(Lights up on **ELLIE**, *down right, talking with* **GUS**. *There are* **BOYS** *and* **GIRLS** *onstage.* **JEFF** *enters right and comes between* **GUS** *and* **ELLIE**.)

JEFF. C'mon, let's go back out there and shake a tailfeather.

ELLIE. Okay. *(They join hands and go center.)*

JASMINE. Jeff… I have dibs on you for this one.

JEFF. *(To* **JASMINE**, *as he is pulled left, away from* **ELLIE**.)* But I just asked her to… *(Turns to* **ELLIE**.)* "Save The Last Dance For Me."

ELLIE. The Drifters, right? *(Music out.)*

JEFF. Right.

ELLIE. Okay, girls, let's show these fellows how to have a party.

> ***[MUSIC NO. 08 "I WANNA LOVE HIM SO BAD"]***
>
> *(This is a* **BOYS** *vs.* **GIRLS** *number. As the* **GIRLS** *sing, the* **BOYS** *huddle off to one side and watch them.)*

CHRISTOPHER. *(Bass singer, on offstage microphone.)*
   BOM BOM BOM BOM BOM BOM

GIRLS & CHRISTOPHER.
   DOWN, DOWN (BOM)
   DOWN, DOWN-BE-DO-BE-DO
   DOWN, DOWN (BOM)
   DOWN, DOWN-BE-DO-BE-DO
   OH…

ELLIE.
   HE LIVES IN MY

GIRLS & CHRISTOPHER.
   NEIGHBORHOOD

ELLIE.
   WHEN HE WALKS BY

GIRLS & CHRISTOPHER.
   HE LOOKS SO GOOD

ELLIE.

WANNA GET TO KNOW HIM

GIRLS & CHRISTOPHER.

…OH, YEAH

ELLIE.

WISH THAT I COULD SHOW HIM

GIRLS.

…I CARE.

ELLIE.	**CHRISTOPHER.**
I WANNA LOVE HIM SO BAD	BOM BOM BOM BOM BOM BOM

GIRLS & CHRISTOPHER.

DOWN, DOWN (BOM)

| YOU KNOW IT'S DRIVIN' ME MAD | DOWN, DOWN-BE-DO-BE-DO |

DOWN, DOWN (BOM)

| 'CAUSE WHEN I LOOK IN HIS… | DOWN, DOWN… |

ELLIE, GIRLS & CHRISTOPHER.

EYES

ELLIE.

I KEEP SEEIN'

ELLIE, GIRLS & CHRISTOPHER.

PARADISE

ELLIE.

OH, I CAN'T HELP IT

I WANNA LOVE HIM SO BAD

GIRLS & CHRISTOPHER.

…LOVE HIM SO BAD

ELLIE.

I KNOW HIS NAME –

ELLIE, GIRLS & CHRISTOPHER.

HIS NAME IS JIM

ELLIE.

I CAN'T BE BLAMED

GIRLS & CHRISTOPHER.

FOR LOVIN' HIM

ELLIE.

I CAN MAKE HIM HAPPY

GIRLS.

…OH, YEAH…

ELLIE.

IF HE'D ONLY LET ME

ELLIE & GIRLS.

…OH, YEAH…

ELLIE.	**CHRISTOPHER.**
I WANNA LOVE HIM SO BAD	BOM BOM BOM BOM BOM BOM

GIRLS & CHRISTOPHER.

DOWN, DOWN (BOM)

	DOWN, DOWN-BE-DO-BE-DO
YOU KNOW IT'S DRIVIN' ME MAD	
	DOWN, DOWN (BOM)
'CAUSE WHEN I LOOK IN HIS…	DOWN, DOWN…

ELLIE, GIRLS & CHRISTOPHER.

EYES

ELLIE.

I KEEP SEEIN'

ELLIE, GIRLS & CHRISTOPHER.

PARADISE

ELLIE.

OH, I CAN'T HELP IT	**ALL.**
I WANNA LOVE HIM SO BAD	OOO

GIRLS & CHRISTOPHER.

…LOVE HIM SO BAD.

(Instrumental under the following, in rhythm.)

ELLIE. How about on a first date?

BARBARA.

NEVER.

JODI.

 HOW ABOUT ON A SECOND DATE?

PATTIE.

 ABSOTIVELY POSITUTELY NOT.

GINA.

 WELL HOW 'BOUT ON A THIRD DATE WHEN HE MEETS
  YOUR PARENTS?

ZORA.

 NOPE.

ELLIE. How about when he's so cute you could die so you really, really have to 'cause it's like a medical emergency?

JASMINE.

 WELL, MAYBE.

ALL.

 AHH.

JASMINE. But keep your eyes open and your lips closed… and whatever you do,

 NEVER LET HIM GO BELOW THE WAIST!

ELLIE. Mickey! You mean "down there"?

	GIRLS & CHRISTOPHER.
ELLIE.	(BOM)
DOWN, DOWN	DOWN, DOWN
YOU KNOW IT'S DRIVIN' ME MAD	DOWN, DOWN-BE-DO-BE-DO
	DOWN, DOWN (BOM)
'CAUSE WHEN I LOOK IN HIS…	DOWN, DOWN…

ELLIE & GIRLS.

 EYES

ELLIE.

 I KEEP SEEIN'

ELLIE, GIRLS & CHRISTOPHER.

 PARADISE

ELLIE.

OH, I CAN'T HELP IT	**GIRLS.**
I WANNA LOVE HIM SO BAD	OOO

GIRLS & CHRISTOPHER.

. . . LOVE HIM SO BAD

[MUSIC NO. 08A "DO WAH DIDDY DIDDY"]

(*The* **BOYS** *break their huddle and chase the* **GIRLS** *from center stage. Now it is the* **BOYS** *' turn.*)

GUS. Come on, boys, let's show 'em how it's done.

JEFF.

THERE SHE WAS

JUST A-WALKIN' DOWN THE STREET SINGIN'

BOYS.

DO WAH DIDDY

DIDDY DOWN DIDDY DO

JEFF.

SNAPPIN' HER FINGERS

AND A-SHUFFLIN' HER FEET SINGIN'

BOYS.

DO WAH DIDDY

DIDDY DOWN DIDDY DO

JEFF.

SHE LOOKED GOOD

BOYS.

YEAH, YEAH

JEFF.

SHE LOOKED FINE

BOYS.

YES SHE DID

JEFF.	**BOYS.**
SHE LOOKED GOOD,	YEAH
SHE LOOKED FINE	YEAH
AND I NEARLY LOST...	YEAH
MY MIND.	

JEFF.

BEFORE I KNEW IT

SHE WAS WALKIN' NEXT TO ME SINGIN'

BOYS.

DO WAH DIDDY

DIDDY DOWN DIDDY DO

JEFF.

SHE WAS HOLDIN' MY HAND
JUST AS NATURAL AS CAN BE SINGIN'

BOYS.

DO WAH DIDDY
DIDDY DOWN DIDDY DO

JEFF.

WE WALKED ON

BOYS.

YEAH, YEAH

JEFF.

TO MY DOOR

BOYS.

SURE DID

JEFF.	**BOYS.**
WE WALKED ON	YEAH
TO MY DOOR	YEAH
AND WE KISSED	YEAH!
A LITTLE MORE	

GIRLS.

MY, MY, MY, MY

BOYS.

WO WO

JEFF.

I KNEW WE WERE FALLIN' IN LOVE

BOYS.

DIT, DIT, DIT, DIT

GIRLS.

MY, MY, MY, MY

JEFF & BOYS.

YES I DID,

JEFF.

SO
I TOLD HER ALL THE THINGS I'VE BEEN DREAMIN' OF

JEFF. **GIRLS.**

   NOW WE'RE TOGETHER   DOWN, DOWN
     NEARLY

   EVERY SINGLE DAY SINGIN'   DOWN, DOWN-BE-DO-BE-DO

BOYS.

   DO WAH DIDDY
   DIDDY DOWN DIDDY DO

JEFF.

   NOW WE'RE SO HAPPY   DOWN, DOWN
   AND NOW IT'S GONNA BE   DOWN, DOWN-BE-DO-BE-DO
   JUST SINGIN'…

BOYS.

   DO WAH DIDDY
   DIDDY DOWN DIDDY DO

JEFF.

   WELL I'M HERS

GIRLS.

   YEAH, YEAH

JEFF.

   AND SHE'S MINE

BOYS.

   YES SHE IS

JEFF. **BOYS.**

   I'M HERS   YEAH
   SHE'S MINE   YEAH
   WEDDING BELLS   YEAH
   ARE GONNA CHIME

BOYS.

   AH…

ALL.

   AH… **JEFF.**
   AH…   WO WO
   AH…   WO YEAH
   DO WAH DIDDY
   DIDDY DOWN DIDDY DO   I'M SINGIN' YEAH
   DO WAH DIDDY   WHOO!
   DIDDY DOWN DIDDY DO

BOYS.	GIRLS.
DO WAH DIDDY	DOWN, DOWN
DIDDY DOWN DIDDY DO	DOWN, DOWN-BE-DO-BE-DO
DO WAH DIDDY	DOWN, DOWN
DIDDY DOWN DIDDY DO	DOWN, DOWN-BE-DO BE-DO
DO WAH DIDDY	DOWN, DOWN
DIDDY DOWN DIDDY DO	DOWN, DOWN-BE-DO-BE-DO
DO WAH DIDDY	DOWN, DOWN
DIDDY DOWN DIDDY DO!	DOWN DIDDY DO!

[MUSIC NO. 08B "I WANNA LOVE HIM SO BAD – CROSSOVER"]

*(All begin to exit except **JEFF** and **ELLIE**. **JEFF** taps **ELLIE** on the shoulder.)*

JEFF. Knock-knock.

ELLIE. Who's there?

JEFF. Astronaut.

ELLIE. Astronaut who?

JEFF. Astronaut what your country can do for you, but what you can do for your country.

> *(**ELLIE** doesn't laugh. **JEFF** thinks it's very funny.)*

ELLIE. Knock-knock.

JEFF. Who's there?

ELLIE. Consumption.

JEFF. Consumption who?

ELLIE. Consumption be done about these lousy jokes you keep telling me?

> *(**ELLIE** laughs as she goes right. **JEFF** follows.)*

JEFF. *(Grabs her by the waist.)* You send me.

[MUSIC NO. 09 "AND THEN HE KISSED ME"]

ELLIE. Sam Cooke, right?

> *(**JEFF** kisses **ELLIE**, and then exits stage right. Immediately from stage right appears a pair of giant lips. Inside the lips stand **JASMINE** and*

PATTIE. ELLIE *joins them. During the song, the lips, with the three* GIRLS *inside, move toward stage left.)*

ELLIE, PATTIE & JASMINE. *(With back-up vocals under.)*
WELL, HE WALKED UP TO ME AND HE ASKED ME IF I
    WANTED TO DANCE
HE LOOKED KINDA NICE AND SO I SAID I MIGHT TAKE A
    CHANCE
AND WHEN WE DANCED HE HELD ME TIGHT
AND WHEN HE WALKED ME HOME THAT NIGHT
ALL THE STARS WERE SHINING BRIGHT
AND THEN HE KISSED ME.

EACH TIME I SAW HIM I COULDN'T WAIT TO SEE HIM AGAIN
I WANTED TO LET HIM KNOW THAT HE WAS MORE THAN A
    FRIEND
I DIDN'T KNOW JUST WHAT TO DO
SO I WHISPERED I LOVE YOU
HE SAID THAT HE LOVED ME TOO
AND THEN HE KISSED ME.

HE KISSED ME IN A WAY THAT I'VE NEVER BEEN KISSED
    BEFORE
HE KISSED ME IN A WAY THAT I WANNA BE KISSED
    FOREVERMORE
OOO...

I KNEW THAT HE WAS MINE SO I GAVE HIM ALL THE LOVE
    THAT I HAD
AND ONE DAY HE TOOK ME HOME TO MEET HIS MOM AND
    HIS DAD
THEN HE ASKED ME TO BE HIS BRIDE
AND ALWAYS BE RIGHT BY HIS SIDE
I FELT SO HAPPY I ALMOST CRIED
AND THEN HE KISSED ME
AND THEN HE KISSED ME
AND THEN HE KISSED ME.

(As the song ends, JEFF *re-enters and* PATTIE *and* JASMINE *exit, leaving* JEFF *kissing* ELLIE, *framed*

by the giant lips. During a blackout, we hear a long, loud kiss.)

[MUSIC NO. 09A "AND THEN HE KISSED ME – CROSSOVER"]

DISC JOCKEY. *(Voice-over.)* That was the kissing tone, and we'll be playing it again a little later on for all you kissin' cousins, so don't tucker out your pucker because it's Friday night, date night, time to grab your steady, Freddy, snuggle up and watch the submarine races 'cause up on Lovers' Lane it's full moon and you all know the name of that tune.

(The lights come up on three COUPLES necking in three parked cars in Lovers' Lane. In the Broadway production, the cars were three flat cutouts attached to short, wheeled stools; a comic effect was achieved by the BOYS sitting on the stools "in" the cars, facing upstage, and the GIRLS straddling them with their legs sticking up in the air. Dim lights and DayGlo costumes completed the mood.)

(JEFF and ELLIE enter from stage left.)

ELLIE. Jeff, what are we stopping here for?

JEFF. There's something that's been on my mind day and night. I mean, it's driving me crazy so we *gotta* do it.

ELLIE. Gee, I dunno, Jeff. I'm not sure… I mean like afterwards, will you still…?

JEFF. Believe me, I wouldn't ask you to do it if I didn't respect you.

(There is a long moan from one of the parked cars.)

ELLIE. Well, I've never done it before.

JEFF. I've never done it in a car.

ELLIE. Okay, let's do it.

JEFF. Okay.

ELLIE. Did you bring it?

JEFF. Yeah, here in my pocket. *(He pulls out a pad and begins writing.)* "My honey does the kissyface…"

ELLIE. Jeff, what is that? What are you doing?

JEFF. Trying to come up with a lyric.

ELLIE. A lyric? You wanted to *write* together? *(Laughing.)* I am so…disappointed.

[MUSIC NO. 10 "HANKY PANKY"]

JEFF. Honey, that's it! *(Hands her the pad and pencil as he runs center.)*

MY BABY DOES THE HANKY PANKY
MY BABY DOES THE HANKY PANKY
MY BABY DOES THE HANKY PANKY
MY BABY DOES THE HANKY PANKY
MY BABY DOES THE HANKY PANKY

I SAW HER WALKIN' ON DOWN THE LINE YEAH

BOYS.

YEAH

JEFF.

YOU KNOW I SAW HER FOR THE VERY FIRST TIME
A PRETTY LITTLE GIRL STANDIN' ALL ALONE
HEY, PRETTY BABY, CAN I TAKE YOU HOME?
I NEVER SAW HER… NEVER EVER SAW HER
MY BABY DOES THE HANKY PANKY

JEFF & MEN.

MY BABY DOES THE HANKY PANKY
MY BABY DOES THE HANKY PANKY
MY BABY DOES THE HANKY PANKY
MY BABY DOES THE HANKY PANKY

("Dance" break: the **GIRLS***' legs, still sticking up in the air, do choreographic movements. Then the* **BOYS** *emerge from the cars, and the* **GIRLS** *"ride" off with the cars.)*

JEFF.

I SAW HER WALKIN' ON DOWN THE LINE, YEAH
YOU KNOW I SAW HER FOR THE VERY FIRST TIME
A PRETTY LITTLE GIRL STANDIN' ALL ALONE
HEY PRETTY BABY CAN I TAKE YOU HOME
I NEVER SAW HER… NEVER EVER SAW HER

MY BABY DOES THE HANKY PANKY
MY BABY DOES THE HANKY PANKY
MY BABY DOES THE HANKY PANKY
YEAH!

[MUSIC NO. 10A "HANKY PANKY" – CROSSOVER]

(The Brill Building.)

*(**ELLIE** is seated at the piano, picking out notes and singing. **GUS** is lying on top of the piano.)*

(Unscored.)

ELLIE.

I REMEMBER WHEN I BROUGHT YOU HOME
I REMEMBER WHAT MY MOMMA SAID

GUS. *(Beats out rhythm.)*

BAP BAP BAP BAP

ELLIE.

DA DA DA DA DA DA DA
SHE TOLD ME THAT MY FACE WAS RED

(Beat.)

GUS. No.

ELLIE.

SHE TOLD ME TO GO BACK TO BED

(Beat.)

GUS. No.

ELLIE.

SHE TOLD ME THAT MY CAT WAS DEAD.

GUS. What?

ELLIE. *(She groans as she gets up from the piano and moves left.)* I remember what my momma said. She said "Get a teaching degree to fall back on." But did I listen?

GUS. *(Falls off the right side of piano.)* No. Don't worry, you'll get it.

*(**ELLIE** throws herself back into the song, using her pen as a microphone.)*

(Unscored.)

ELLIE.

> I REMEMBER WHEN I BROUGHT YOU HOME
> I REMEMBER WHAT MY MOMMA SAID
> BAP BAP BAP BAP

JEFF. *(Enters left, runs to* **ELLIE,** *taking pen out of her hand.)*

> WHEN I TOLD HER THAT I LOVED YOU
> SHE TOLD ME I WAS OUT OF MY HEAD

ELLIE. *(Throwing herself at his feet.)* Yes! Thank you!

GUS. *(At piano.)* Don't stop go on, go on!

JEFF. What about marriage?

ELLIE. *(Rises.)* No.

JEFF. No?

GUS. No, we're –

> NOT TOO YOUNG, YOUNG TO GET MARRIED.

> *(Goes left to* **JEFF.***)* Jeff, you're a genius! You solved the whole problem of the hook!

JEFF. I did? *(Back to* **ELLIE.***)* Honey, I'm talking about you – and me – eternally!

ELLIE. Man and wife?

JEFF. For the rest of my life.

GUS. This is not a lyric.

ELLIE. Oh, I have to think about it. *(A beat.)* I've thought about it.

JEFF. And?

ELLIE. Okay!

JEFF. Okay! *(They kiss.)*

GUS. Okay!

ELLIE. I love you, Jeffrey Barry.

JEFF. I love you, Eleanor Louise Greenwich.

> *(***JEFF** *pulls* **ELLIE** *with him right. He sits on the piano stool and pulls her onto his lap.)*

GUS. I'd love to know how many times we repeat the chorus.

ELLIE. As many times as Jeff likes.

> *[MUSIC NO. 11 "NOT TOO YOUNG TO GET MARRIED"]*
>
> *(They kiss. Lights down on them as* **DARLENE,** **PATTIE,** *and* **GINA** *enter right, wearing "sack" dresses.)*

DARLENE.

> MY MAMA SAID I CAN'T SEE YOU NO MORE
> 'CAUSE WE DON'T KNOW WHAT LOVE REALLY MEANS.
> SHE SAYS WE CAN'T GET MARRIED FOR THREE YEARS OR
>   MORE
> 'CAUSE WE'RE ONLY IN OUR TEENS.
>
> OH NO WE'RE

DARLENE, PATTIE & GINA.

> NOT TOO YOUNG, YOUNG TO GET MARRIED
> NOT TOO YOUNG, YOUNG TO GET MARRIED
> WHAT KINDA DIFFERENCE CAN A FEW YEARS MAKE
> I GOTTA HAVE YOU NOW OR MY HEART WILL BREAK
> NOT TOO YOUNG, YOUNG TO GET MARRIED
> NOT TOO YOUNG, YOUNG TO GET MARRIED
> I COULDN'T LOVE YOU MORE THAN I DO TODAY.

> *(***ENSEMBLE** *sings back-up vocals from offstage.)*

DARLENE.

> I REMEMBER WHEN I BROUGHT YOU HOME
> I REMEMBER WHAT MY MAMA SAID
> WHEN I TOLD HER THAT I LOVED YOU SO
> SHE TOLD ME I WAS OUTTA MY HEAD.
> OH, NO WE'RE

DARLENE, PATTIE & GINA.

> NOT TOO YOUNG, YOUNG TO GET MARRIED
> NOT TOO YOUNG, YOUNG TO GET MARRIED
> WHAT KINDA DIFFERENCE COULD A FEW YEARS MAKE
> I GOTTA HAVE YOU NOW OR MY HEART WILL BREAK
> NOT TOO YOUNG, YOUNG TO GET MARRIED
> NOT TOO YOUNG, YOUNG TO GET MARRIED
> I COULDN'T LOVE YOU MORE THAN I DO TODAY.

(Instrumental.)

DARLENE. *(Back-up vocals offstage.)*
GONNA LOVE YOU TILL THE DAY I DIE
WANNA SPEND EVERY DAY WITH YOU
DON'T THEY KNOW HOW THEY MAKE ME CRY
WHEN THEY CARRY ON LIKE THEY DO

OH, NO WE'RE

DARLENE, PATTIE & GINA.
NOT TOO YOUNG, YOUNG TO GET MARRIED
NOT TOO YOUNG, YOUNG TO GET MARRIED
WHAT KIND OF DIFFERENCE COULD A FEW YEARS MAKE
I GOTTA HAVE YOU NOW OR MY HEART WILL BREAK
NOT TOO YOUNG, YOUNG TO GET MARRIED
NOT TOO YOUNG, YOUNG TO GET MARRIED
I COULDN'T LOVE YOU MORE THAN I DO TODAY

ALL. *(***DARLENE*** riffs.)*
NOT TOO YOUNG, YOUNG TO GET MARRIED
NOT TOO YOUNG, YOUNG TO GET MARRIED
NOT TOO YOUNG, YOUNG TO GET MARRIED

DOO DOO
DOO DOO DOO
DOO DOO DOO DOO DOO

[MUSIC NO. 12 "CHAPEL OF LOVE"]

*(***DARLENE, PATTIE***, and ***GINA****'s sack dresses fall down, transforming into full-length bridesmaid outfits. We are at ***ELLIE*** and ***JEFF****'s wedding. The ***ENSEMBLE*** enters – the ***GIRLS*** dressed as bridesmaids, the ***BOYS*** as ushers – in pairs, including ***ROSIE*** and ***GUS*** as a couple. ***JEFF*** and ***ELLIE*** enter as bride and groom, and cross down the "aisle" formed by the ***ENSEMBLE***. The mood is solemn and church-like.)*

GIRLS.
GOIN' TO THE CHAPEL AND WE'RE
GONNA GET MARRIED
GOIN' TO THE CHAPEL AND WE'RE

GONNA GET MARRIED
GEE, I REALLY LOVE YOU AND WE'RE
GONNA GET MARRIED
GOIN' TO THE CHAPEL OF LOVE

SPRING IS HERE
THE SKY IS BLUE
WO, BIRDS ALL SING
AS IF THEY KNEW
TODAY'S THE DAY
WE'LL SAY I DO
AND WE'LL NEVER BE LONELY ANYMORE...
BECAUSE WE'RE

GOIN' TO THE CHAPEL AND WE'RE
GONNA GET MARRIED
GOIN' TO THE CHAPEL AND WE'RE
GONNA GET MARRIED
GEE, I REALLY LOVE YOU AND WE'RE
GONNA GET MARRIED
GOIN' TO THE CHAPEL OF LOVE

> *(Dance. For the dance break, the mood suddenly switches from sacred to wild 60s, and then back to the church again.)*

BELLS WILL RING
THE SUN WILL SHINE
WO, I'LL BE HIS
AND HE'LL BE MINE
WE'LL LOVE UNTIL
THE END OF TIME
AND WE'LL NEVER BE LONELY ANYMORE

DARLENE.

YEAH, YEAH, YEAH, YEAH

LADIES.

GOIN' TO THE CHAPEL OF LOVE

PATTIE.

YEAH, YEAH, YEAH, YEAH

GIRLS & BOYS.

GOIN' TO THE CHAPEL OF LOVE.

> *[MUSIC NO. 12A "CHAPEL OF LOVE – CROSSOVER"]*

> *(Brill Building.)*

> *(JEFF and ELLIE are locked in an embrace. GUS comes left to them, carrying his jacket. It is as if GUS has virtually interrupted the wedding.)*

> *[MUSIC NO. 13 "SONGWRITING MEDLEY"]*

GUS. All right, it's time to work! Come on, kids, the honeymoon is over. This is the music business – one day you write it, the next day you record it and the next week, it's on the radio! Come on, give me a song!

> *(JEFF goes to the piano, sits down, and plays. ELLIE follows JEFF and holds to his left. From stage left, PATTIE and PETER enter, carrying a mike. DARLENE and CHRISTOPHER enter right with a microphone.)*

JEFF & ELLIE.

BOMP SHU BOMP
BOMP SHU BOMP
BOMP SHU BOMP
BOMP

GUS.

WHAT?

ELLIE.

I HAVE A...

JEFF.

I HAVE A...

GUS.

I HAVE A...

PATTIE.   **OTHERS.**

I HAVE A BOY FRIEND   OH OH OH OH OH OH OH

OH   BOMP

    (Music continues under.)

GUS. I love it! Five hundred thousand copies sold! Great backgrounds! *(Jumps to top of piano and stretches out.)* Now give me another one!

ELLIE.

    I MET HIM ON A SUNDAY.

JEFF. *(Swings on piano stool to her.)* The Shirelles did "Met Him On A Sunday."

ELLIE.

    I MET HIM ON A MONDAY.

GUS. And what happened?

ELLIE. *(Arms around* **JEFF.** *)*

    AND MY HEART STOOD STILL.

GUS. Sounds good!

JEFF & ELLIE.

    DA DOO RON RON... RON

    We'll fill in the rest later.

GUS. Record it. (**GUS** *goes left.)*

GROUP.

    DA DOO RON RON RON

    DA DOO RON RON

    DA DOO RON RON RON

    DA DOO RON RON

GUS. That's a great lyric! Give me another one!

    (**GUS** *lies on the floor of a left platter, feet up on a pole.)*

JEFF.

    BOM DO BE DO WOP

JEFF & ELLIE.

    BOM DE DO

ELLIE.

    OH WHO OH OH

GROUP.

    BOM DO BE DO WOP BOM DE DO

OH WHO OH OH

ELLIE. I can't believe we're getting paid for having this much fun!

GUS. *(Sits up on stage floor.)* Would you stop having so much fun and write me another!

JEFF & ELLIE.

BOW BOW BOW DIDIT

DIDIT

DIDIT

DIT

GROUP.

BOW BOW BOW DIDIT (DIT)

DIDIT (DIT)

DIDIT

WE OOH BOW BOW DIDIT (DIT)

DIDIT (DIT)

DIDIT

WE OOH...

GUS. I don't understand a word you're saying, but it sells! You've got seven in the top twenty! I want a Ronettes tune – something as great as "Be My Baby."

> *(**PETER** and **PATTIE** exit left. **DARLENE** and **CHRISTOPHER** exit right. **JEFF** and **ELLIE** are at the piano. **GUS** is downstage, talking to the orchestra as if he is "mixing" sound.)*

> *[MUSIC NO. 14 "BABY I LOVE YOU"]*

I love it! I love it! That's it! Now give me more bass... drums...timpani...guitar...horns...echo! Press it! Release it!

> *(**GUS** exits left. **JEFF** carries **ELLIE** off right.)*

> *(**ANNIE**, **BARBARA**, and **JASMINE** enter right. They wear round-bottomed "hoop" skirts which, when turned up, resemble enormous 45 RPM records with their legs as the center spindles.)*

ANNIE.

WO, OH

WO, OH, OH, OH.

HAVE I EVER TOLD YOU
HOW GOOD IT FEELS TO HOLD YOU
IT ISN'T EASY TO EXPLAIN

ANNIE.	GIRLS.
AND THOUGH I'M REALLY TRYIN'	AH…
I THINK I MAY START CRYIN'	AH…
MY HEART CAN'T WAIT ANOTHER DAY	AH…
WHEN YOU KISS ME I JUST GOT TO SAY	AH…

GIRLS.

BABY I LOVE YOU

ANNIE.

COME ON BABY

GIRLS.

BABY I LOVE YOU

ANNIE.

OO WEE BABY

GIRLS.

BABY I LOVE ONLY YOU…

ANNIE.

…BABY I LOVE ONLY YOU
WO, OH… WO, OH, OH, OH.

ANNIE.	GIRLS.
I CAN'T LIVE WITHOUT YOU	OOOO…
I LOVE EVERYTHING ABOUT YOU	OOOO…
I CAN'T HELP IT IF I FEEL THIS WAY	OOOO…
OH, I'M SO GLAD I FOUND YOU	AH…
I WANT MY ARMS AROUND YOU	AH…
I LOVE TO HEAR YOU CALL MY NAME	AH…
OH TELL ME THAT YOU FEEL THE SAME	AH…

GIRLS.

BABY I LOVE YOU

ANNIE.

COME ON BABY

GIRLS.

BABY I LOVE YOU

ANNIE.

OO WEE BABY

GIRLS.

BABY, I LOVE ONLY YOU.

ANNIE.

...BABY, I LOVE ONLY YOU

WO, OH... WO, OH, OH, OH.

GIRLS.

OOOO...

OOOO

OOOO...

OOOO...

AH

ANNIE.

COME ON, BABY

GIRLS.

BABY I LOVE YOU

ANNIE.

OO WEE BABY

GIRLS.

BABY I LOVE YOU

ANNIE.

COME ON BABY

GIRLS.

BABY I LOVE ONLY YOU...

ANNIE.

...BABY I LOVE ONLY YOU

COME ON, COME ON, COME ON, BABY

GIRLS.

BABY I LOVE YOU

ANNIE.

OO WEE BABY

LADIES.

BABY I LOVE YOU

ANNIE.

COME ON BABY

GIRLS.

BABY, I LOVE...

ANNIE.

BABY, I LOVE

ANNIE & GIRLS.

ONLY YOU

ANNIE.

WO, OH... WO, OH, OH, OH...

> ### *[MUSIC NO. 14A "BABY I LOVE YOU – CROSSOVER"]*
>
> *(**ELLIE** enters left with a sheet of music and pen. **JEFF** enters left in a motorcycle outfit. He crosses behind her, reaches over her shoulders, and takes her arms, holding them as if they were on a motorcycle.)*
>
> ### *[MUSIC NO. 14B "AFTER BABY I LOVE YOU"]*

JEFF. Right turn...left turn... Hey, honey – look at the royalty check we just got.

ELLIE. *(Barely looking.)* Oh, that's great. I can get my roots done.

JEFF. Yeah, get your roots done. I just bought a new motorcycle.

ELLIE. For twenty-eight dollars? Did it come with batteries?

JEFF. Twenty-eight dollars? Twenty-eight dollars? Look again. *(Takes check from pocket.)*

ELLIE. *(She looks.)* Twenty-eight thousand dollars, oh my God! *(They embrace.)*

JEFF. *(Pulls* **ELLIE** *right.)* Come on, let's celebrate! I'll take you for a ride before I pack.

ELLIE. Pack? Pack for where?

JEFF. Gus wants to produce the new single in L.A.

ELLIE. *(Excited.)* L.A.? We're going to sunny California?

JEFF. No, honey, I'm going to L.A. I need to do this alone.

ELLIE. What are you saying to me?

(Both go center, hand in hand.)

JEFF. That you gotta stop doing so much. One day soon we're going to have a family and you'll be staying home anyway, so I might as well start now building my name as the producer.

ELLIE. What about my name?

JEFF. *(Putting his hands on her waist.)* Well, your name is my name. You're Mrs. Jeff Barry.

ELLIE. *(Pulls away.)* I'm also Ellie Greenwich.

JEFF. You'll still get the writing credit.

ELLIE. I'm also a producer. I'm doing the vocals for the Ronettes' new tune, I'm working on the rhythm track for the Dixiecups, and even as we speak, I'm late for a string date with the Jelly Beans.

JEFF. *(Tries to take music from her.)* From now on I'll take care of those things.

ELLIE. *(Pulls music away.)* How? By riding around on a motorcycle pretending you're James Dean? There's enough work around here for two, Jeffrey.

JEFF. Wrong, Eleanor – because you won't stop trying to do it all! I'm going home to pack 'cause I'm going to L.A.

(He starts to exit.)

ELLIE. Jeff, wait! Don't leave. Don't.

JEFF. *(Stops, turns back to her.)* "Don't" Elvis, 1957.

(He exits right.)

ELLIE. *(Yelling after him.)* 1958!

(GUS enters left, carrying a canvas traveling bag and some music.)

GUS. Hi, Ellie. Ready to work? *(Puts bag on floor.)*

ELLIE. Wouldn't you rather work with Jeff? He's the one you're taking to L.A.

GUS. Look, it wasn't my idea to do this one without you.

ELLIE. But Gus, we've always done everything together.

GUS. Maybe it's best you stay home 'cause I need you to write. We've got the session booked and the release date, but what we don't have is a new song for the Shangri-Las. So will you get busy and do it?

ELLIE. *(Takes sheet music from GUS.)* All right, I'll do it.

GUS. *(Giving her a kiss.)* See you when we get back.

(He picks up his bag and exits right.)

ELLIE. *(As she exits right.)* Gus… I hope it rains for the entire trip!

[MUSIC NO. 15 "LEADER OF THE PACK"]

*(The **GIRLS** enter stage left, dressed as motorcycle molls in skin-tight pedal-pusher pants, heeled boots, and corset tops, with tall beehive hairdos and long ponytails.)*

*(From upstage, in a huge cloud of smoke, the **GUYS** enter. They are dressed as motorcycle gang members and hold handlebars with headlights to suggest that they are on bikes The combination of handlebars, smoke, and sound effects gives us the impression that they are "riding" toward the audience.)*

(Offstage vocals under the following.)

JASMINE. Is she really goin' out with him?

BARBARA. I don't know…let's ask her.

JASMINE & BARBARA. Hey, Betty, is that Jimmy's ring you're wearing?

ANNIE.

UH, HUH.

SHIRLEY. Gee it must be great riding with him. Is he picking you up after school today?

ANNIE.

UH, HUH

ALL GIRLS.

BY THE WAY, WHERE'D YOU MEET HIM?

ANNIE.

I MET HIM AT THE CANDY STORE
HE TURNED AROUND AND SMILED AT ME
YOU GET THE PICTURE?

GIRLS.

...YES, WE SEE

ANNIE.

THAT'S WHEN I FELL FOR

ANNIE & GIRLS.

THE LEADER OF THE PACK

(Vroom, vroom, vroom, vroom.)

(The **GUYS** *spread out, and the* **GIRLS** *join the* **GUYS** *on their "cycles" and "ride" behind them.)*

ANNIE.

MY FOLKS WERE ALWAYS PUTTING HIM DOWN

GIRLS.

DOWN, DOWN

ANNIE.

THEY SAID HE CAME FROM THE WRONG SIDE OF TOWN

GIRLS.

WHAT YOU MEAN WHEN YOU SAY THAT
HE CAME FROM THE WRONG SIDE OF TOWN?

ANNIE.	**GIRLS.**
THEY TOLD ME HE WAS BAD	OOO...
BUT I KNEW HE WAS SAD	OOO...

THAT'S WHY I FELL FOR...   OOO...

ANNIE & GIRLS.

THE LEADER OF THE PACK

(Vroom, vroom, vroom, vroom.)

ANNIE.

ONE DAY MY DAD SAID "FIND SOMEONE NEW"

I HAD TO TELL MY JIMMY, "WE'RE THROUGH"

GIRLS.

WHAT YOU MEAN WHEN YOU SAY THAT

YOU BETTER GO FIND SOMEBODY NEW?

ANNIE.	**GIRLS.**
HE STOOD THERE AND ASKED ME WHY	OOO...
BUT ALL I COULD DO WAS CRY	OOO...
I'M SORRY I HURT YOU	OOO...

ANNIE & GIRLS.

THE LEADER OF THE PACK

(Dance. The GIRLS get off the "cycles." The GUYS park their "cycles" and dance with the GIRLS. At the conclusion of the dance, the GUYS "ride" off, leaving the GIRLS to continue the song.)

ANNIE.	**GIRLS.**
He sorta smiled and kissed me goodbye.	DO, DO, DO...
The tears were beginning to show.	DO, DO, DO...
As he drove away on that rainy night	DO, DO, DO...
I begged him to go slow.	DO, DO, DO...
Whether he heard... I'll never know.	DO, DO, DO...
	DO, DO, DO...
	NO, NO, NO, NO,
LOOK OUT!	NO,
LOOK OUT!	NO,

LOOK OUT!   NO!
LOOK OUT!

> *(Offstage crash.)*

ANNIE.

I FELT SO HELPLESS WHAT COULD I DO
REMEMBERIN' ALL THE THINGS WE'D BEEN THROUGH
IN SCHOOL THEY ALL STOP AND STARE
I CAN'T HIDE THE TEARS… BUT I DON'T CARE
I'LL NEVER FORGET HIM…

ANNIE & GIRLS.

THE LEADER OF THE PACK

> *(Vroom, vroom, vroom, vroom.)*

> *(The **GUYS** re-enter, minus one.)*

GIRLS.

GONE…

ANNIE.

LEADER OF THE PACK NOW HE'S GONE

GIRLS.

…GONE, GONE, GONE, GONE, GONE, GONE…

ANNIE.

LEADER OF THE PACK NOW HE'S GONE

GIRLS.

GONE…

ANNIE.

LEADER OF THE PACK NOW HE'S GONE

GIRLS.

…GONE, GONE, GONE, GONE, GONE, GONE…

ANNIE.

LEADER OF THE PACK NOW HE'S GONE

GIRLS.

GONE…

ANNIE.

LEADER OF THE PACK NOW HE'S GONE

GIRLS.

…GONE, GONE, GONE, GONE, GONE, GONE…

ANNIE.

LEADER OF THE PACK NOW HE'S GONE...

GIRLS.

GONE...

ANNIE.

LEADER OF THE PACK NOW HE'S GONE

GIRLS.

...GONE, GONE, GONE, GONE, GONE, GONE.

[MUSIC NO. 15A "LEADER OF THE PACK – CROSSOVER"]

(In its final version, the Broadway production was performed without intermission. However, an intermission may be placed at this point if desired.)

(JEFF *and* **ELLIE** *are down right, finishing dressing.)*

ELLIE. So how many awards are we getting? Tell me again.

JEFF. Six.

ELLIE. Six! That's three more than last year.

JEFF. Does that mean I'm supposed to be twice as happy?

ELLIE. Sure!

JEFF. Then I'm not feeling what I'm supposed to be feeling.

ELLIE. Jeffrey, this year we've won twice the awards, made three times as much money and moved from Lefrak City to Central Park West. What more could you want?

JEFF. I want to start a family.

[MUSIC NO. 15B "AFTER LEADER OF THE PACK – DRESSING SCENE"]

ELLIE. Right now? Don't you think we should wait until after the awards ceremony?

JEFF. We're twenty-four years old and I'd like to start living like normal people.

ELLIE. So we'll buy a Chevrolet.

JEFF. You see, everytime I get serious – you make a wisecrack.

ELLIE. Jeff, I want a family, too. But this isn't the right time.

JEFF. Four years and it's never been "the right time" with you.

ELLIE. We have sessions booked. There's Darlene's single. There's so much more we should do before we raise a family.

JEFF. When I try to talk about us, you always end up talking about business – or is that all we are, a business?

ELLIE. Jeff, can't this wait until later?

JEFF. I don't want to wait any longer.

ELLIE. *(Puts her arm through his.)* Well, you'll have to because it's time to go. So tell me. Do I look like a person who's about to accept half a dozen awards?

JEFF. You look like you're wearing the wallpaper from some steakhouse. Come on.

[MUSIC NO. 16 "BE MY BABY – SWING"]

(JEFF exits right. ELLIE follows.)

(The lights come up on a nightclub. The sign "Chez Smooch" hangs over the downstage platter, upstage of a floor mike. On the stage floor, center and left, are several COUPLES dancing.)

[MUSIC NO. 16A "CHEZ SMOOCH: CHA-CHA'S"]

VOICE-OVER. Ladies and gentlemen, we invite you to join us at Chez Smooch for an evening of dining, dancing and great entertainment. So sit back and relax with the one you love.

(From up right we hear laughter as GUS and ELLIE enter, carrying their awards. JEFF follows. All are wearing dark glasses. The entrance is applauded by the DANCERS.)

ELLIE. *(Pointing right.)* Hey, get a load of the ice sculpture by the bar.

JEFF. That's not an ice sculpture – that's Andy Warhol.

ELLIE. *(Going to the lips banquette right.)* Do you think we're supposed to sit on these lips?

GUS. Do you want me to check your awards? I'm going to dance with mine.

> *(Takes awards from* **ELLIE** *and goes left, joining a group of people.)*

JEFF. Ellie, we've got our awards. Let's go home.

ELLIE. *(Sits on the lips.)* Jeff, I want to talk.

JEFF. *(Sits to her right, thinking she means about them.)* Oh... great. It's about time.

ELLIE. About some new ideas.

JEFF. New ideas?

ELLIE. We're going to have to come up with a lot of new ideas if we're going to stay on top.

JEFF. We're at the top. We just won six awards.

ELLIE. The Beatles won ten. Just because the world suddenly wants Lennon and McCartney doesn't necessarily mean it's the end of Greenwich and Barry.

JEFF. Barry and Greenwich. Tell me, Ellie...do you really love me or do you love writing songs with me?

ELLIE. What are you talking about? It's the same thing.

JEFF. But if you had to choose...would it be me or the music?

ELLIE. I love you both.

WAITRESS.* *(Coming to the left of them.)* Hi...can I get you a cocktail?

JEFF. I'm asking you to make a choice.

ELLIE. Jeff, I don't know how to choose.

WAITRESS. All right, I'll give her a little more time.

> *(She leaves.)*

JEFF. You don't know? Well, if that's your answer...you don't know what's more important...then maybe we should quit while we're ahead.

---

* Either a CHORUS MEMBER, or played by JASMINE.

ELLIE. Quit what? What are you saying?

JEFF. Maybe we ought to split up.

ELLIE. You want to write with someone else?

WAITRESS. *(Coming to them.)* Do you folks know what you want?

ELLIE. Jeff, answer me.

JEFF. This is not an easy decision to make.

WAITRESS. Oh, that's okay. I'll give him a little more time.

> *(She leaves again.)*

JEFF. I've been thinking about moving to L.A. There's a big future in writing movie scores.

ELLIE. L.A.? Movie scores? I thought you were telling me you wanted to write with someone else...now you're telling me you want to get into the movies?

JEFF. What I'm trying to tell you is...I think we should get a divorce.

ELLIE. A divorce?

JEFF. I'm sorry, Ellie.

ELLIE. Jeff, is that really what you want?

WAITRESS. *(Returning with a camera.)* How about a photo?

JEFF. Yes, that's really what I want.

> *(**WAITRESS** snaps photo.)*

> *(**PATTIE** comes to the microphone on the platter.)*

[MUSIC NO. 17 "LOOK OF LOVE"]

PATTIE.
> LOOK AT THE WAY HE LOOKS AT HER
> LOOK AT THE WAY HE SMILES
> I REMEMBER WHEN HE WAS MINE
> I REMEMBER WHEN THINGS WERE FINE
> OH, LOOK AT THE WAY HE LOOKS AT HER NOW
> ISN'T THAT THE LOOK OF LOVE?
> OOO...
> LOOK OF LOVE
>
> LOOK AT THE WAY HE HOLDS HER HAND

LOOK AT THE WAY THEY DANCE
I REMEMBER WHEN HE LOVED ME
I REMEMBER HOW IT USED TO BE
BUT LOOK AT THE WAY HE SMILES AT HER NOW
ISN'T THAT THE LOOK OF LOVE
OOO...
LOOK OF LOVE

> (**JEFF** *starts to rise.* **ELLIE** *puts her arm on his arm in hopes of keeping him. He leaves.*)

PATTIE.

HERE I AM ALL BY MYSELF
WATCHING HIM WITH SOMEONE ELSE
BET HE DOESN'T EVEN KNOW I'M HERE
WISH I COULD HOLD BACK MY TEARS
THE TEARS...

> (**ELLIE** *exits right.*)

> (*One of the dancing* **COUPLES** *performs a balletic pas de deux, showing great passion between two lovers, echoing the previous scene. Their dance fades into normal ballroom dancing as* **PATTIE**'s *vocal resumes.*)

OHH... OOO...
OHH... OOO...
THE LOOK OF LOVE
THE LOOK OF LOVE... OOO...

LOOK AT THE WAY HE'S KISSING HER
LOOK AT HIM HOLDING HER TIGHT
I REMEMBER HIS WARM EMBRACE
AND THE TENDER LOOK ON HIS FACE, YES
LOOK AT THE WAY HE LOOKS AT HER NOW
ISN'T THAT THE LOOK OF LOVE
ISN'T THAT
ISN'T THAT
THE LOOK OF WOAH... WOAH...
ISN'T THAT THE LOOK OF...
LOVE...?

> (*The dancing* **COUPLES** *embrace. The scene fades.*)

[MUSIC NO. 17A "LOOK OF LOVE – CROSSOVER"]

*(**SHELLEY** enters right and walks over to **ELLIE**, who is addressing Christmas cards.)*

SHELLEY. Hi, honey.

ELLIE. Hi, Shelley!

SHELLEY. How ya doin'?

ELLIE. I'm fine. The eggnog's made, the tree's up, the dreidel's spinning…everything's fine.

SHELLEY. *(Taking cards from **ELLIE**.)* Ellie, what is this? *(Reading one, then another.)* "From Ellie Greenwich and Jeffy Barry " "Love, Ellie and Jeff." Honey, you're divorced.

ELLIE. *(Taking the cards back.)* I know, but it's the holidays. People don't want to hear bad news.

SHELLEY. Ellie, you don't have to pretend with me. I've known you since we were Jivettes. Remember?

ELLIE. "We don't smoke and we don't bet…"

SHELLEY. Not "bet," we didn't pet.

ELLIE. Maybe you didn't.

ELLIE & SHELLEY. "But we're the hippest you can get We're not jive – we're just Jivettes."

*(**ELLIE** breaks down.)*

ELLIE. Oh, Shelley, I miss him so bad.

(Blackout.)

[MUSIC NO. 18 "CHRISTMAS – BABY PLEASE COME HOME"]

*(**DARLENE, JASMINE,** and **GINA** appear, dressed as "Santa's helpers." They sing in front of a giant Christmas stocking.)*

GIRLS & BASS.

CHRISTMAS
CHRISTMAS
CHRISTMAS
CHRISTMAS

CHRISTMAS…

DARLENE.

THE SNOW'S COMIN' DOWN

JASMINE & GINA.

CHRISTMAS…

DARLENE.

I'M WATCHIN' IT FALL

JASMINE & GINA.

CHRISTMAS…

DARLENE.

LOTS OF PEOPLE AROUND

JASMINE & GINA.

CHRISTMAS…

DARLENE.

BABY PLEASE COME HOME

JASMINE & GINA.

CHRISTMAS…

DARLENE.

THE CHURCH BELLS IN TOWN

JASMINE & GINA.

CHRISTMAS…

DARLENE.

ARE RINGIN' A SONG

JASMINE & GINA.

CHRISTMAS…

DARLENE.

WHAT A HAPPY SOUND

JASMINE & GINA.

CHRISTMAS…

DARLENE.

BABY PLEASE COME HOME

JASMINE & GINA.

OOO…

DARLENE.

THEY'RE SINGIN' DECK THE HALL
BUT IT'S NOT LIKE CHRISTMAS AT ALL

'CAUSE I REMEMBER WHEN YOU WERE HERE
AND ALL THE FUN WE HAD LAST YEAR

JASMINE & GINA.

CHRISTMAS...

DARLENE.

PRETTY LIGHTS ON THE TREE

JASMINE & GINA.

CHRISTMAS...

DARLENE.

I'M WATCHIN' THEM SHINE

JASMINE & GINA.

CHRISTMAS...

DARLENE.

YOU SHOULD BE HERE WITH ME

JASMINE & GINA.

CHRISTMAS...

DARLENE.

BABY PLEASE COME-A HOME

JASMINE & GINA.

OOO...

THEY'RE SINGIN' DECK THE HALL
BUT IT'S NOT LIKE CHRISTMAS AT ALL
'CAUSE I REMEMBER WHEN YOU WERE HERE
AND ALL THE FUN WE HAD LAST YEAR

JASMINE & GINA.

CHRISTMAS...

DARLENE.

IF THERE WAS A WAY

JASMINE & GINA.

CHRISTMAS...

DARLENE.

I'D HOLD BACK THESE TEARS

JASMINE & GINA.

CHRISTMAS...

DARLENE.

BUT IT'S CHRISTMAS DAY

JASMINE & GINA.
 PLEASE
DARLENE.
 PLEASE
JASMINE & GINA.
 PLEASE
DARLENE.
 PLEASE
JASMINE & GINA.
 PLEASE
DARLENE.
 PLEASE
JASMINE & GINA.
 PLEASE
DARLENE.
 PLEASE
JASMINE & GINA.
 PLEASE
DARLENE.
 PLEASE
JASMINE & GINA.
 PLEASE
DARLENE.
 PLEASE
JASMINE & GINA.
 PLEASE

DARLENE.	**JASMINE & GINA.**
BABY PLEASE COME HOME	PLEASE, PLEASE,

JASMINE & GINA.
 CHRISTMAS...
DARLENE.
 BABY PLEASE COME HOME
JASMINE & GINA.
 CHRISTMAS...
DARLENE.
 BABY PLEASE COME HOME

JASMINE & GINA.

CHRISTMAS…

DARLENE.

BABY PLEASE COME HOME

JASMINE & GINA.

CHRISTMAS…

DARLENE.

OH YEAH, YEAH, YEAH…

DARLENE.	**JASMINE & GINA.**
YEAH…	CHRISTMAS…

[MUSIC NO. 18A "CHRISTMAS – BABY PLEASE COME HOME – CROSSOVER"]

*(The scene is now a recording studio. As the lights come up, **GUS** is onstage wearing a headset. **ELLIE** enters up center.)*

GUS. Ellie! Long time no see.

ELLIE. Have you seen Jeff?

GUS. He's around someplace. *(He tries to hug her, but she pulls away.)* So how are you doing? I meant to phone, but what could I say?

ELLIE. "Hello. Sorry I haven't called in two years."

GUS. I have thought about you. Ellie, I was real sorry to hear about your mom.

ELLIE. Well, it hasn't been the best of times. I do thank you for getting Jeff back to New York. It feels good to be working again.

GUS. I wanted a couple of hits, but I thought maybe you two could work out the rest

ELLIE. I'm giving it time. Time? Funny thing is all the time Jeff and I were together our timing was all off.

GUS. And now?

ELLIE. So far we haven't talked about us. We'll get around to it.

GUS. I hope so.

ELLIE. So did Jeff give you the new songs?

GUS. They're sensational. I think we should record "River Deep Mountain High" with Tina Turner.

ELLIE. Tina? I love Tina, but Darlene really wants that song.

GUS. I've got other songs for Darlene. And right now we're getting set up to do the demo of "I Can Hear Music."

ELLIE. You don't waste any time, do you?

> (**KEITH** *enters down right carrying a microphone. He puts it in the center of the downstage platter.* **ANNIE**, **JEFF**, **PATTIE**, *and* **LON** *approach the mike from upstage.* **KEITH** *joins the group.*)

GUS. Time is money.

ELLIE. So let's do it.

[MUSIC NO. 19 "I CAN HEAR MUSIC"]

> (**GUS** *and* **ELLIE** *go right to the platter. They remain on the stage floor.*)

ANNIE.

THIS IS THE WAY	
I ALWAYS DREAMED IT	
WOULD BE	**BACK-UP SINGERS.**
THE WAY THAT IT IS	HA HA HA HA
OH YEAH	
WHEN YOU ARE HOLDING	AHH
ME	
I NEVER HAD	
A LOVE OF MY OWN	
MAYBE THAT'S WHY	
WHEN WE'RE ALL ALONE	
I CAN HEAR MUSIC	OOO...
I CAN HEAR MUSIC	OOO...

> (**JEFF** *leaves the group on the platter and joins* **ELLIE** *and* **GUS** *on the stage floor.* **JEFF** *has a headset.*)

THE SOUND OF THE CITY	OOO
BABY	
SEEMS TO DISAPPEAR	OOO

(AND OH) I CAN HEAR MUSIC	OOO
SWEET, SWEET MUSIC	AHH
WHENEVER YOU TOUCH ME BABY...	AH, OOO
WHENEVER YOU'RE NEAR.	OOO

JEFF. That's great, Annie.

GUS. Sounds like a good one. Let me play around with the background vocals.

    *(He joins the **BACK-UP SINGERS** on the platter.)*

    (On the stage floor, there is an awkward moment.)

ELLIE. *(Feeling good.)* So...here we are, back in the old recording studio...just like we used to be...almost.

ANNIE & BACK-UP SINGERS.

    I HEAR THE MUSIC HOLD ME TIGHT, YEAH

ELLIE. It's good having you back in New York, Jeff.

JEFF. Yeah... I've missed it.

ELLIE. And it's missed you. *(Trying to make light of this.)* And what the hell – just say it – I've missed you.

JEFF. I've missed you, too, Ellie. *(They embrace.)*

ANNIE & BACK-UP SINGERS.

    I HEAR THE MUSIC HOLD ME TIGHT NOW BABY

ELLIE. *(Pulls away, really excited.)* Oh, Jeff...somehow I just knew we'd get back together. I mean, we were young and made a lot of mistakes – but now that's all over with. I've got so many ideas for songs we can do. You know me, never out of ideas.

JEFF. That sounds great, but I've got to catch a plane back to the coast.

ELLIE. *(Not understanding.)* So when are you coming back?

ANNIE & BACK-UP SINGERS.

    I HEAR THE MUSIC HOLD ME TIGHT

JEFF. *(Goes left.)* I have a life out there now.

ANNIE & BACK-UP SINGERS.

    I HEAR THE MUSIC

JEFF. I've got a house with a backyard and plenty of room. It's not as exciting as New York, but it's home and we like it.

ELLIE. We?

ANNIE & BACK-UP SINGERS.

I HEAR THE SWEET SWEET MUSIC

JEFF. Ellie, I'm getting married.

ELLIE. *(Trying to cover her feelings.)* I wish you all the happiness in the world, Jeffrey.

JEFF. Thanks.

ELLIE. *(Trying not to break.)* It was nice working with you again.

JEFF. *(Backs off left.)* Well, so long.

ELLIE. "So Long"…Fats Domino, right?

JEFF. Right.

> *(The music builds and* **JEFF** *exits.* **ELLIE** *stays onstage.)*

ANNIE & BACK-UP SINGERS.

I CAN HEAR MUSIC

I CAN HEAR MUSIC

THE SOUND OF THE CITY BABY

ANNIE.

SEEMS TO DISAPPEAR

ANNIE & BACK-UP SINGERS.

I CAN HEAR MUSIC

SWEET, SWEET MUSIC

BACK-UP SINGERS.

OOO, TOUCH ME, BABY

WHENEVER YOU'RE NEAR

ANNIE.

WHENEVER YOU TOUCH ME BABY…

WHENEVER YOU'RE NEAR

WHENEVER YOU TOUCH ME BABY…

WHENEVER YOU'RE NEAR

BACK-UP SINGERS.

I HEAR THE MUSIC,

HEAR THE
ANNIE & BACK-UP SINGERS.
SWEET, SWEET MUSIC.

> *(The* **BACK-UP SINGERS** *exit. The microphone is taken off.* **ELLIE** *remains, alone.)*

[MUSIC NO. 20 "ROCK OF RAGES"]

ELLIE.

NO, I'M NOT DOIN' VERY WELL
I BUILT A LOT OF DREAMS BUT THEY FELL DOWN TWO BY
  TWO
YES IT'S TRUE…

I NEVER THOUGHT HE'D SAY GOODBYE
BUT WHEN THE MUSIC CHANGED I FELT THE MAGIC DIE
OH, WHY… OH, WHY?

YEAH, WE WERE STANDIN' AT THE TOP
BUT THE PANIC WOULDN'T STOP
AND THE CHAPEL OF LOVE FELL DOWN
WITH THE ENGLISH BEAT ALL AROUND

I DON'T WANNA TURN THE PAGES…
ROCK OF RAGES…

OH MAMA I'M CALLIN'
BUT NO ONE LISTENS TO ME ANYMORE
OH DADDY – I'M FALLIN'
AND PLEASE CATCH ME LIKE YOU DID BEFORE.

OH, NOW I'M BARELY HANGIN' ON
YOU KNOW THE FEAR RUSHED IN WHEN THE INNOCENCE
  WAS GONE
IT WAS GONE. CAN'T GO ON

I TRIED TO SLEEP AWAY THE PAIN
I CAN'T KEEP THE TEARS FROM FALLIN' LIKE THE RAIN
IT'S INSANE… ALL THIS PAIN – OOO YEAH

I WAS HIDING
MY WORLDS COLLIDING
AND THE LEADER OF THE PACK WENT DOWN, DOWN
IS SHE EVER COMIN' BACK TO TOWN?

I DON'T WANNA TURN THE PAGES...
ROCK OF RAGES...

MAMA, I MISS YOU WANNA BE WITH YOU
MAMA YOU ALWAYS KNEW HOW TO HELP ME
DADDY, I MISS YOU – WANNA BE WITH YOU
WISH YOU COULD COME BACK JUST FOR A LITTLE WHILE

OH, MAMA – I'M BREAKIN'
PLEASE TAKE ME AND HOLD ME IN YOUR ARMS TONIGHT
AND DADDY – I'M SHAKIN'
PLEASE WAKE ME AND TELL ME EVERYTHIN'S ALL RIGHT.

[MUSIC NO. 20A "ELLIE'S ENTRANCE"]

(The lights on stage fade out.)

*(This moment and music in the Broadway production marked the entrance of the real **ELLIE GREENWICH**. **YOUNG ELLIE** remained in a spotlight. As she turned and began slowly walking up center, a beam of light came up through a door up center, which had opened The real **ELLIE GREENWICH** entered, walked downstage, and met **YOUNG ELLIE** She put her hand on **YOUNG ELLIE**'s shoulder for a brief moment Then **ELLIE GREENWICH** came downstage as **YOUNG ELLIE** exited up center. The up center door closed and the lights came up full onstage.)*

*(Productions without the real **ELLIE GREENWICH** may use this moment, and "Ellie's Entrance Music," to show **ELLIE**'s transition from her nervous breakdown in "Rock Of Rages" to the recovered, confident star she is today, in whatever manner the director sees fit. The same actress may play **ELLIE** throughout the show, or an older actress may take over at this transitional point.)*

[MUSIC NO. 21 "DA DOO RON RON"]

*(The full **COMPANY** enters, now back in the 1980s and wearing their costumes from the opening of the show.)*

ELLIE & ALL. *(Shouting.)* One-two-
One-two-three-four-

ELLIE.
I MET HIM ON A MONDAY AND MY HEART STOOD STILL

ELLIE & ALL.
DA DOO RON RON RON
DA DOO RON RON

ELLIE.
SOMEBODY TOLD ME THAT HIS NAME WAS BILL

ELLIE & ALL.
DA DOO RON RON RON
DA DOO RON RON

YES... MY HEART STOOD STILL
YES... HIS NAME WAS BILL
AND WHEN HE WALKED ME HOME
DA DOO RON RON RON
DA DOO RON RON

ELLIE.
HE KNEW WHAT HE WAS DOIN' WHEN HE CAUGHT MY EYE

ELLIE & ALL.
DA DOO RON RON RON
DA DOO RON RON

ELLIE.
HE LOOKED SO QUIET BUT MY OH MY

ELLIE & ALL.
DA DOO RON RON RON
DA DOO RON RON

YES... HE CAUGHT MY EYE
YES... BUT MY OH MY
AND WHEN HE WALKED ME HOME
DA DOO RON RON RON
DA DOO RON RON

(Dance.)

ELLIE.
HE PICKED ME UP AT SEVEN AND HE LOOKED SO FINE

ELLIE & ALL.
>DA DOO RON RON RON
>DA DOO RON RON

ELLIE.
>SOMEDAY SOON I'M GONNA MAKE HIM MINE

ELLIE & ALL.
>DA DOO RON RON RON
>DA DOO RON RON
>
>YES... HE LOOKED SO FINE
>YES... I'M GONNA MAKE HIM MINE
>AND WHEN HE WALKED ME HOME
>DA DOO RON RON RON
>DA DOO RON RON

ALL. *(A cappella.)*
>DA DOO RON RON RON
>DA DOO RON RON
>DA DOO RON RON RON
>DA DOO RON RON

ELLIE.	**ALL.**
YEAH, YEAH,	DA DOO RON RON RON
YEAH, YEAH,	DA DOO RON RON
YEAH, YEAH,	DA DOO RON RON RON
YEAH, YEAH,	DA DOO RON RON

(Music back in.)

OH, I LOVE HIM	DA DOO RON RON RON
AND I NEED HIM	DA DOO RON RON
I'M GONNA KEEP HIM	DA DOO RON RON RON
BY MY SIDE	DA DOO RON RON
YEAH...	DA DOO RON RON RON
OH WOAH...	DA DOO RON RON
DA DOO RON RON RON	DA DOO RON RON RON
DA DOO RON RON	DA DOO RON RON

ELLIE. I can't believe that it took my music twenty-three years to get from the Brill Building at 49th and Broadway to the Ambassador Theatre at Broadway and 49th.

PATTIE. Ellie, could I ask you a question? "Da Doo Ron Ron" is so great – but what does it mean?

ELLIE. Nothing.

PATTIE. Everything means something.

ELLIE. That is true. But this time, it means absolutely nothing. We'd be writing these songs and when we'd get stuck for a line we'd throw in these little riffs. Even to this day Jeff and I will speak and he'll say, "You know, Ellie, we could have gone...and when he walked me home, we had a cup of coffee and we watched TV." And I go, "And when he walked me home, we had a glass of wine and then he jumped on me." There's a lot of things you can do other than "da doo ron ron."

DANNY. Yeah, but did you do...

DOWN, DOOBIE DOO DOWN DOWN?

ELLIE. No, I didn't. I did...

DOWN, DOWN,
DOWN, DOWN-BE-DO-BE-DO

ELLIE & ALL.

DOWN, DOWN,
DOWN, DOWN-BE-DO-BE-DO
OH...

(**JOEY** *raises his hand as he gets up from the floor where he was sitting.*)

ELLIE. Yes, Mouseketeer?

JOEY. Weren't you once in a group called "The Raindrops"?

ELLIE. Yes. I was The Raindrops. I did all the voices.

JOEY. *All* the voices? Even...

[MUSIC NO. 22 "WHAT A GUY"]

BOW-BOW-BOW...

ELLIE. No, that one was Jeff.

JOEY.

DIDIT DIDIT DIDIT
DIT BOW-BOW-BOW
DIDIT DIDIT DIDIT

MEN.

DIT BOW-BOW-BOW...

ELLIE.   **BOYS.**

I...   DIDDIT DIDDIT...

SEE HIM EVERY DAY   *(Continues throughout.)*

HE PASSED MY WAY

WHAT CAN I DO?

OH, OH, OH WHAT A GUY

OH, OH, OH, OH WHAT A
     GUY

WHAT A GUY – HE'S SWEET
     AND GENTLE

WHAT A GUY – HE'S
     SENTIMENTAL

WHAT A GUY

OH, OH, OH HERE HE
     COMES AGAIN

HE'LL SMILE AND THEN

SHOULD I SMILE TOO?

WO, OH, OH WHAT A GUY

OH, OH, OH, OH WHAT A
     GUY

WHAT A GUY – HIS HAIR IS
     WAVY

WHAT A GUY – HE DRIVES
     ME CRAZY

WHAT A GUY

I WANNA TELL HIM

YEAH – TELL HIM

I LOVE HIM – OH YEAH

TELL HIM THAT I REALLY
     CARE

GIVE HIM ALL MY LOVE TO
     SHARE

WANT HIM SO MUCH I
     COULD DIE

YEAH, YEAH, YEAH

HE'S THE ONLY GUY FOR
    ME
BUT WHO'S THE HUNK IN
    THE BALCONY?
WHAT A GUY – WHAT A GUY
I LOVE HIM SO
BUT WHO'S THE DOLL IN
    THE SECOND ROW?
WHAT A GUY – WHAT A GUY
WHAT A GUY

GIRLS.

HOOT

BOYS.

DIDIT

ALL.

WHAT A GUY!

ELLIE. Darlene, you and I have been waiting a long time for this one. Take it! "River Deep, Mountain High."

[MUSIC NO. 24 "RIVER DEEP MOUNTAIN HIGH"]

(**ELLIE** *exits left.*)

DARLENE.

WHEN I WAS A LITTLE GIRL I HAD A RAGDOLL
THE ONLY DOLL I EVER OWNED
NOW I LOVE YOU JUST THE WAY I LOVED THAT RAGDOLL
BUT ONLY NOW MY LOVE HAS GROWN
AND IT GETS STRONGER

ENSEMBLE.

STRONGER

DARLENE.

IN EVERY WAY
AND IT GETS DEEPER, BABY

ENSEMBLE.

DEEPER

DARLENE.

AND LET ME SAY

AND IT GETS HIGHER

ENSEMBLE.

HIGHER

DARLENE.

DAY BY DAY

ENSEMBLE.

DO I LOVE YOU, MY, OH, MY
RIVER DEEP, MOUNTAIN HIGH
IF I LOST YOU WOULD I CRY?
OH HOW I LOVE YOU, BABY BABY, BABY, BABY...

DARLENE. *(Back-up vocals under.)*

WHEN YOU WERE A YOUNG BOY DID YOU HAVE A PUPPY
THAT ALWAYS FOLLOWED YOU AROUND?
WELL, I'M GONNA BE AS FAITHFUL AS THAT PUPPY
NO, I'LL NEVER LET YOU DOWN
'CAUSE IT GOES ON AND ON

ENSEMBLE.

ON AND ON

DARLENE.

LIKE A RIVER FLOWS
AND IT GETS BIGGER BABY

ENSEMBLE.

BIGGER

DARLENE.

AND HEAVEN KNOWS
THAT IT GETS SWEETER, BABY

ENSEMBLE.

SWEETER

DARLENE.

AS IT GROWS... OH

DARLENE & ENSEMBLE.

DO I LOVE YOU, MY, OH, MY
RIVER DEEP, MOUNTAIN HIGH
IF I LOST YOU WOULD I CRY?
OH HOW I LOVE YOU BABY BABY,
BABY, BABY

DARLENE. *(Back-up under.)*

I LOVE YOU BABY
LIKE A FLOWER LOVES THE SPRING
AND I LOVE YOU BABY
LIKE A ROBIN LOVES TO SING
I LOVE YOU BABY
LIKE THE SCHOOLBOY LOVES HIS PIE
I LOVE YOU BABY,
RIVER DEEP, MOUNTAIN HIGH

DARLENE.	**ENSEMBLE.**
YEAH, YEAH, YEAH, YEAH	AH…
YEAH, YEAH, YEAH, YEAH	AH…
YEAH, YEAH, YEAH, YEAH	AH…
YEAH, YEAH, YEAH, YEAH	AH…

DARLENE & ENSEMBLE.

DO I LOVE YOU MY OH MY

DARLENE.

I LOVE YOU BABY… I LOVE YOU

ENSEMBLE.

RIVER DEEP, MOUNTAIN
    HIGH

(DARLENE riffs.)

IF I LOST YOU WOULD I
    CRY?

DARLENE.

I LOVE YOU BABY… I LOVE YOU

ENSEMBLE.

OH HOW I LOVE YOU BABY
BABY, BABY, BABY

> *[MUSIC NO. 25 "WE'RE GONNA MAKE IT AFTER ALL"]*

ELLIE. *(Entering from left.)* Darlene, that was worth every minute waiting to hear you sing that. You know… I love the old songs, but here's one that I've written for now…for all of us.

WE'RE GONNA MAKE IT AFTER ALL
'CAUSE AFTER ALL, LOOK WHAT WE'VE BEEN THROUGH
WE'RE GONNA TAKE IT TO THE SKY
WE'RE REACHING HIGH, THE WAY WE USED TO DO.

ANNIE.

> SAY GOODBYE TO ALL THE TEARS AND SORROW
> AND LET'S RECALL THE JOYS AND SPECIAL MEM'RIES OF
>   THE PAST
> HOLD ONTO THE MAGIC OF TOMORROW
> AND LET'S MAKE THIS MOMENT LAST.

DARLENE.

> WE'RE GONNA MAKE IT TO THE END
> YOU'RE MY BEST FRIEND AND I'M SO PROUD OF YOU
> WE'RE GONNA TAKE IT ALL THE WAY
> THIS TIME WE'LL STAY BECAUSE WE WANTED TO.

ELLIE.

> NEVER BE AFRAID OF
>   WHERE YOU'RE GOIN'

ANNIE.	**ENSEMBLE.**
NO MATTER HOW	*(Underneath)*
IMPOSSIBLE THE ROAD	OOO
AHEAD MAY SEEM	

DARLENE.

JUST FEEL THE STRENGTH	AHH!
INSIDE YOU KEEP ON	
GROWIN'	

ELLIE, ANNIE & DARLENE.

AND JUST HANG ONTO	HANG ONTO YOUR DREAM
YOUR DREAM.	

ALL.

> TONIGHT WE'LL MAKE UP

DARLENE.

> FOR THE TIME WE LOST

ALL.

> OOO...

DARLENE.

> WE'LL NEVER BREAK UP – NOT AT ANY COST

ELLIE.

> I CAN FEEL FOREVER

ELLIE, ANNIE & DARLENE.

> I CAN FEEL IT COMIN' TOGETHER

ALL.

WE'RE GONNA MAKE IT
OH, OH-OH, OH WO-O-OH
WE'RE GONNA MAKE IT-OH

GIRLS.

'TIL THE END

BOYS.

'TIL THE END

ALL.

MY BEST FRIEND
OH, OH-OH, OH
WO-O-OH
WE'RE GONNA MAKE IT

NEVER BE AFRAID OF WHERE YOU'RE GOIN'
NO MATTER HOW IMPOSSIBLE THE ROAD AHEAD MAY SEEM
FEEL THE STRENGTH INSIDE YOU KEEP ON GROWIN'
AND JUST HANG ONTO YOUR DREAM.

ELLIE.

A… MY NAME IS ELLIE
AND MY MAMA'S NAME IS MUSIC

> *(If separate actresses play* **ELLIE** *and* **YOUNG
> ELLIE,** *then* **YOUNG ELLIE** *appears down left with
> her accordion.)*

YOUNG ELLIE.

I COME FROM A PLACE CALLED LEVITTOWN

ELLIE & YOUNG ELLIE.

WHERE I SANG MY SONGS
AND MY MAMA HELPED ME WRITE 'EM DOWN

> *(***YOUNG ELLIE** *exits down left.)*

ALL.

WE'RE GONNA MAKE IT AFTER ALL.

> *[MUSIC NO. 26 "BOWS"]*

> *[MUSIC NO. 27 "EXIT MUSIC"]*

> *(Curtain Call Reprise.)*

ALL. *(Shouting.)* One – two –
　　One – two – three – four –
　　　DO I LOVE YOU, MY, OH, MY
　　　RIVER DEEP, MOUNTAIN HIGH
　　　IF I LOSE YOU WOULD I CRY?
　　　OH HOW I LOVE YOU, BABY,
　　　BABY, BABY, BABY.

OPTIONAL MUSIC – KEEP IT CONFIDENTIAL

(The following song originally came after "Rock of Rages" and before "Da Doo Ron Ron." On April 17, 1985, nine days after opening night, it was cut from the show. At the director's option, the song may be used between the aforementioned songs, left out of the show, or perhaps used as the opening of Act II, if an intermission is inserted.)

GINA.

IF A MAN CAN LOVE A LIAR
AND A WOMAN CAN LOVE A THIEF
THERE'S A FEW THINGS BABY
YOU SHOULD KNOW ABOUT ME
I'VE ALWAYS LOOKED FOR POWER
IN ALL THE LOVERS I KNEW
BUT NOW I KNOW THE GLORY
OF SIMPLY LOVIN' YOU

YOU SEE... I WON'T PLAY THE OLD CHARADE

GIRLS.

I WON'T PLAY THE OLD CHARADE

GINA.

IT'S TIME TO STOP THE MASQUERADE

GIRLS.

IT'S TIME TO STOP THE MASQUERADE

GINA.

WHY DON'T YOU STRIP ME BARE

GIRLS.

FEEL IT

GINA.

AND FEEL THE TRUTH

GIRLS.

FEEL IT

GINA.

THAT'S ALL I'VE GOT TO GIVE TO YOU

GIRLS.

GIVE TO YOU.

GINA.

WHY DON'T YOU TAKE THESE SECRETS
BUT KEEP 'EM CONFIDENTIAL

GINA & GIRLS.

STRICTLY CONFIDENTIAL

GINA & BARBARA.

KEEP IT CONFIDENTIAL

GIRLS. Strictly confidential.

GINA.

KEEP IT STRICTLY

GINA & GIRLS.

CONFIDENTIAL

GINA.

LOVIN' YOU BABY IS ON MY MIND YOU BETTER

GIRLS.

KEEP IT

GINA.

KEEP IT

GIRLS.

KEEP IT

GINA.

KEEP IT
LOVIN' YOU BABY IS ON MY MIND

GIRLS.

LOVIN' YOU BABY IS ON MY MIND

GINA.

YOU BETTER KEEP IT

GIRLS.

KEEP IT

GINA.

OOO...

I WOULD CALL YOU LOVER
BUT I USED THAT NAME BEFORE

GINA & GIRLS.

LIVIN' UNDERCOVER

GINA.

ALWAYS KEEPIN' SCORE

BUT THERE'S A FEW THINGS 'BOUT YOU BABY
THAT'S BREAKIN' THIS CHAIN OF LIES

GIRLS.

NO ONE ELSE COULD MAKE ME

GINA.

NO ONE ELSE COULD MAKE ME
OPEN UP MY...

GINA & GIRLS.

EYES

GINA.

YOU SEE... I WON'T PLAY THE OLD CHARADE

GIRLS.

I WON'T PLAY THE OLD CHARADE

GINA.

TIME TO STOP THE MASQUERADE

GIRLS.

TIME TO STOP THE MASQUERADE

GINA.

WHY DON'T YOU STRIP ME BARE

GIRLS.

FEEL IT

GINA.

AND FEEL THE TRUTH

GIRLS.

FEEL IT

GINA.

THAT'S ALL I'VE GOT TO GIVE TO YOU

GIRLS.

GIVE TO YOU

GINA.

WHY DON'T YOU TAKE THESE SECRETS
BUT KEEP 'EM CONFIDENTIAL

GINA & GIRLS.

STRICTLY CONFIDENTIAL

GINA & BARBARA.

    KEEP IT CONFIDENTIAL

GIRLS. Strictly confidential.

GINA.

    KEEP IT STRICTLY

GINA & GIRLS.

    CONFIDENTIAL

    OOO...

       (Dance.)

GINA.

    LOVIN' YOU BABY IS ON MY MIND

    YOU BETTER

GIRLS.

    KEEP IT

GINA.

    KEEP IT

GIRLS.

    KEEP IT

GINA.

    LOVIN' YOU BABY IS ON MY MIND

    YOU BETTER

GIRLS.

    KEEP IT

GINA.

    KEEP IT

    LOVIN' YOU BABY IS ON MY MIND

GIRLS.

    LOVIN' YOU BABY IS ON MY MIND

    YOU BETTER

GINA.

    KEEP IT

GIRLS.

    KEEP IT

GINA.

    KEEP IT

GIRLS.

KEEP IT

GINA.

KEEP IT

GIRLS.

KEEP IT

GIRLS.	**GINA.**
KEEP, KEEP IT CONFIDENTIAL	OH…
KEEP, KEEP IT CONFIDENTIAL	
KEEP IT, KEEP IT	CONFIDENTIAL

ALL.

YOU BETTER KEEP IT!

MUSICAL TIMINGS

Dance Opening		2:22
BE MY BABY		2:32
WAIT 'TIL MY BOBBY GETS HOME		2:06
A… MY NAME IS ELLIE		:36
JIVETTE BOOGIE BEAT		:55
WHY DO LOVERS BREAK EACH OTHER'S HEARTS		2:43
TODAY I MET THE BOY I'M GONNA MARRY		2:35
I WANNA LOVE HIM SO BAD		
	vocals	1:31
	dialogue	:31
	vocals	:20
		2:22
DO WAH DIDDY DIDDY		1:44
AND THEN HE KISSED ME		1:50
HANKY PANKY		2:18
HANKY PANKY playoff		:22
NOT TOO YOUNG TO GET MARRIED		1:57
CHAPEL OF LOVE		2:54
BABY I LOVE YOU		2:37
BABY I LOVE YOU playoff		:19
LEADER OF THE PACK		4:39
LOOK OF LOVE		
	vocal	1:29
	dance	1:35
	vocal	:44
		3:48
CHRISTMAS – BABY PLEASE COME HOME		2:19
I CAN HEAR MUSIC		
	vocal	:58
	dialogue	1:47
	vocal	:49
		3:34
ROCK OF RAGES		2:46
DA DOO RON RON		2:01
WHAT A GUY		1:28
RIVE DEEP, MOUNTAIN HIGH		3:29
WE'RE GONNA MAKE IT AFTER ALL		3:44
Bows		2:04
Music played after bows		:46

COSTUME PLOT

(refers to the original cast:)

JEFF .... Patrick Cassidy
ANNIE .... Annie Golden
ELLIE .... Ellie Greenwich
DARLENE .... Darlene Love
YOUNG ELLIE .... Dinah Manoff
PRODUCER (GUS) .... Dennis Bailey

Female Back-up Singers
1. Jodi Moscia
2. Pattie Darcy
3. Jasmine Guy
4. Zora Rasmussen
5. Gina Taylor
6. Barbara Yeager
7. Shirley Black-Brown

Male Back-up Singers
1. Keith McDaniel
2. Peter Neptune
3. Joey Scheck
4. Chris Gregory
5. Danny Herman
6. Lon Hoyt

Opening Dance
Female Back-up Singers
1. Black sequin dress, black net hose, black shoes
3. Black sequin dress, black net hose, black shoes
7. Black sequin dress, black net hose, black shoes

Male Back-up Singers
1. Black dance pants, sequin top, black shoes
3. Black dance pants, sequin top, black shoes
4. Black dance pants, sequin top, black shoes
5. Black dance pants, sequin top, black shoes

Dialogue
Darlene – teal blue beaded top, silk pants, shoes, rhinestone jewelry

Be My Baby
Annie – green & white lace top, calypso pants, gold shoes, jewelry

Female Back-up Singers
1. Repeat opening costume
2. Green & white lace top, calypso pants, gold shoes & jewelry

3. Repeat opening costume
6. Green & white lace top, calypso pants, gold shoes & jewelry
7. Repeat opening costume

Male Back-up Singers
1. Repeat opening costume
3. Repeat opening costume
4. Repeat opening costume
5. Repeat opening costume

Dialogue
Darlene – repeat teal opening costume

Wait 'Til My Bobby Gets Home
Darlene – repeat teal opening costume

Female Back-up Singers
1. Repeat opening costume
5. Black sequin dress, black hose, black shoes
7. Repeat opening costume

Male Back-up Singers
1. Repeat opening costume
2. Black dance pants, sequin top, black shoes
3. Repeat opening costume
5. Repeat opening costume
6. Black dance pants, sequin top, black shoes

Dialogue
Darlene – repeat teal opening costume

A… My Name is Ellie
Young Ellie – yellow eyelet dress, black & white checked collar and apron, cream shoes

Levittown & Jivette Boogie Beat
Young Ellie – repeat yellow dress

Female Back-up Singers
3. Yellow eyelet dress, black & white checked collar and apron, cream shoes
4. Grey silk shirtwaist dress, red print smock, red slippers
6. Yellow eyelet dress, black & white checked collar and apron, cream shoes

Writers' Crossover
Jeff – beige & pink polo shirt, chinos, tan shoes

Male Back-up Singers
1. Grey pants, black shirt, yellow wool jacket
2. Red pants, red ruffled shirt, bow tie, black shoes, grey wool jacket
3. Blue pants, blue shirt, grey jacket, black shoes
6. Grey pants, grey shirt, green H.S. letter sweater, black shoes, black beret

Brill Building
Jeff – repeat first costume
Producer (Gus) – cream check pants, yellow shirt, rust jacket, print scarf, brown suede shoes
Young Ellie – yellow dress with music applique skirt, blue sweater, pink belt & shoes

Why Do Lovers Break Each Other's Hearts
Darlene – pink & black strapless gown, black shoes, black jewelry

Female Back-up Singers
2. Blue & black skirt, white top dress, yellow belt, black shoes
5. Blue & black skirt, white top dress, yellow belt, black shoes

Male Back-up Singer
3. Blue & black striped pants, white jacket with gold ascot, black shoes

Bomp Shu Bom
Jeff – yellow pants, yellow shirt, yellow argyle sweater vest, tan shoes
Young Ellie – coral skirt & blouse & shoes

Party & Today I Met The Boy I'm Gonna Marry
Producer – brown pants, yellow shirt, brown tie, brown suede vest, green jacket, brown shoes, orange scarf
Jeff – repeat yellow outfit
Darlene – tomato red beaded satin dress and shoes, crystal jewelry
Young Ellie – repeat coral skirt & blouse

Female Back-up Singers
1. Red & grey checked skirt, beige blouse, grey belt, beige shoes
2. Cranberry plaid skirt, tan sweater, green velour vest, cranberry shoes
3. Brown skirt, gold sweater, leopard print vest & shoes
6. Brown sweater, teal blue skirt and belt, teal blue shoes & scarf
7. Green skirt, beige sweater, orange vest, tan belt & shoes

Male Back-up Singers
1. Rust shirt, burgundy pants, brown jacket, black shoes
2. Green pants, orange shirt, green sweater vest, black shoes
3. Brown pants, green shirt, maroon velour vest, black shoes
5. Green pants, brown pullover top with orange dickey, black shoes
6. Gold pants & vest, yellow & brown shirt, tie, black shoes

I Wanna Love Him So Bad
Young Ellie – repeat coral outfit

Female Back-up Singers
1. Repeat party costume
2. Repeat party costume
3. Repeat party costume
4. Rust jumper, green cardigan, rust print scarf, brown shoes
5. Gold plaid skirt, gold blouse, green sweater, brown shoes
6. Repeat party costume
7. Repeat party costume

Do Wah Diddy
Jeff – repeat party costume
Producer – repeat party costume

Male Back-up Singers
1. Repeat party costume
2. Repeat party costume
3. Repeat party costume
4. Repeat party costume
5. Repeat party costume
6. Repeat party costume

Knock Knock – And Then He Kissed Me
Young Ellie – repeat party costume
Jeff – repeat party costume

Female Back-up Singers
2. Repeat party costume
3. Repeat party costume
5. Repeat party costume

Male Back-up Singer
6. Repeat party costume

Lovers' Lane
Jeff – blue jeans, white sleeveless sweater, white sneakers
Young Ellie – white bathing suit top with blue pedal pushers, sandals,
    white sweater

Female Back-up Singers
1. Grey pants, black & green leotard, pink boots
6. Grey pants, green tube top, green boots
7. Grey pants, pink & orange stretch top, orange shoes

Male Back-up Singers
1. Grey jeans, black & orange body suit, black shoes
3. Grey jeans, black & pink body suit, black shoes
5. Grey jeans, black & green body suit, black shoes

Hanky Panky
Jeff – repeat lovers lane costume

Male Back-up Singers
1. Repeat lovers lane costume
3. Repeat party costume
5. Repeat party costume

Brill Building (Marriage Proposal)
Young Ellie – pastel madras dress, pink belt, sandals
Producer – black pants, purple shirt, black & white tie, purple print
    jacket, black shoes

Female Back-up Singer
7. Jeans, white sweater, peach windbreaker

Not Too Young to get Married
Darlene – pink satin sheath with bubble overshirt, lace gloves, pink
    shoes, hair wreath

Female Back-up Singers
2. Pink satin sheath, bubble overshirt, lace gloves, pink shoes, hair
    wreath
5. Pink satin sheath, bubble overshirt, lace gloves, pink shoes, hair
    wreath

Chapel of Love
Producer – maroon jacket, black pants, white formal shirt, maroon tie
Jeff – white tie and tails
Darlene – repeat pink sheath with long skirt Young Ellie – wedding gown
    & veil

Female Back-up Singers
1. Pink satin sheath with long overskirt, lace gloves, pink shoes, head
    wreath, floral ball
2. Repeat pink sheath & long skirt
3. Pink satin sheath with long overskirt, lace gloves, pink shoes, head
    wreath, floral ball
4 Green silk gown & jacket, lavender hat/bag/shoes
5. Repeat pink sheath with long skirt
6. Pink satin sheath with long overskirt, lace gloves, pink shoes, head
    wreath with floral ball
7. Pink sheath with long overskirt, lace gloves, pink shoes, head wreath
    with flower ball

Male Back-up Singers
1 Black pants, white shirt, black bowtie and cummerbund, yellow
    jacket, black shoes

2   Black pants, white shirt, black bowtie and cummerbund, yellow jacket, black shoes
3   Black pants, white shirt, black bowtie and cummerbund, yellow jacket, black shoes
5   Black pants, white shirt, black bowtie and cummerbund, yellow jacket, black shoes

Medley

Producer – white shirt & bowtie, black pants, checked suspenders, purple cummerbund

Jeff – white tie and tails

Young Ellie – wedding gown and veil

Darlene – pink sheath with blue linen jacket, pink shoes

Female Back-up Singer

2. Pink sheath dress with blue linen jacket, pink shoes

Male Back-up Singers

2. Black pants, white shirt, blue satin baseball jacket
4. Black pants, white shirt, blue satin baseball jacket

Baby I Love You

Producer – repeat medley costume

Annie – red tulle and gold lame dress, black stretch pants, gold shoes

Female Back-up Singers

3. Red tulle and gold lame record dress, black stretch pants, gold shoes
6. Red tulle and gold lame record dress, black stretch pants, gold shoes

Motorcycle scene

Producer – yellow shorts, red Hawaiian shirt, pink tie & hat, yellow bag, beige suede shoes and socks

Jeff – black leather jacket, green slacks, blue polo shirt, tan loafers

Young Ellie – pink halter dress, white belt, white shoes

Leader of the Pack

Annie – gold pants, lace stockings, gold belt, silver boots, red leather jacket

Female Back-up Singers

1. Black boots, 2 tone stretch pants & corset
3. Black boots, rose and purple stretch pants & corset
6. Black boots, 2 tone stretch pants & corset
7. Black boots, green & purple stretch pants & corset

Male Back-up Singers

1. Black pants, leather jacket & gloves, black shoes, green mesh shirt
3. Black pants, leather jacket & gloves, black shoes, red mesh shirt
4. Black pants, leather jacket & gloves, black shoes, pink mesh top

5. Black pants, leather jacket & gloves, black shoes, green mesh top
6. Black pants, leather jacket & gloves, black shoes, purple mesh top

Dressing scene
Jeff – Tux – formal shirt, patent shoes
Young Ellie – black & red wallpaper print silk dress, black satin belt, red sequin shoes

Chez Smooch – Look of Love
Producer – white shirt, black pants, purple tie & cummerbund, plaid jacket, black shoes
Jeff – repeat tux
Young Ellie – repeat black & red dress

Female Back-up Singers
1. Pink crepe & lace dress, pink shoes
2. Magenta silk dress, rhinestone trim, black shoes
3. Black dress with applique flowers, black shoes
5. Black sheath, black shoes
6. Turquoise chiffon sheath, beige shoes
7. Pink & lavender chiffon dance dress, nude sandals

Male Back-up Singers
1. Black pants, black vest, purple shirt, bowtie, blackshoes
2. Black pants, white shirt, brown jacket, bowtie
3. Black pants, white shirt, bowtie, green jacket, black shoes
5. Black pants, white shirt, bowtie, maroon jacket
6. Black pants, white shirt, bowtie, blue jacket, black shoes

Christmas Card scene
Young Ellie – pale yellow robe, blue slippers
Female Back-up Singer
6. Blue/green tweed coat, black shoes, blue/green pillbox hat

Christmas – Baby Please Come Home
Darlene – red Santa jacket, short skirt, hat, white maribou trim, white boots

Female Back-up Singers
3. Red Santa jacket, short skirt, hat, white maribou trim, white boots
5. Red Santa jacket, short skirt, hat, white maribou trim, white boots

Reunion Scene
Producer – rust jacket, yellow shirt, brown tie, rust & yellow pants, brown shoes
Young Ellie – black suede miniskirt, pink suede top, black shoes

I Can Hear Music
Producer – repeat reunion costume
Jeff – beige slacks, blue cotton sweater, tan loafers
Annie – taupe suede dress, grey striped linen jacket, grey shoes
Young Ellie – repeat reunion costume

Female Back-up Singer
2. Brown plaid cotton skirt, beige jacket & scarf, beige shoes

Male Back-up Singers
1. Cream shirt, khaki pants, beige tweed jacket
6. Grey wool pants, cream striped sweater, grey shirt

Rock of Rages – Ellie's Entrance
Ellie – black sequin pants, hot pink beaded top, black shoes
Young Ellie – repeat reunion costume

Keep It Confidential
Female Back-up Singers
1. Beige trench coat, hat, shoes, black net hose, briefs
3. Beige trench coat, hat, shoes, black net hose, briefs
5. Grey trench coat, hat, shoes, black net hose, briefs
6. Beige trench coat, hat, shoes, black net hose, briefs
7. Beige trench coat, hat, shoes, black net hose, briefs

Male Back-up Singers
1. Navy trench coat, hat, white scarf, black dance pants, shoes
3. Navy trench coat, hat, white scarf, black dance pants, shoes
4. Navy trench coat, hat, white scarf, black dance pants, shoes

Da Doo Ron Ron, Dialogue, What a Day
Ellie – repeat pink & black costume

Female Back-up Singers
1. Repeat opening black sequin dance costume
2. Repeat opening black sequin dance costume
3. Repeat opening black sequin dance costume
4. Repeat opening black sequin dance costume
5. Repeat opening black sequin dance costume
6 Repeat opening black sequin dance costume
7. Repeat opening black sequin dance costume

Male Back-up Singers
1. Repeat opening black sequin dance costume
2. Repeat opening black sequin dance costume
3. Repeat opening black sequin dance costume
4. Repeat opening black sequin dance costume
5 Repeat opening black sequin dance costume
6. Repeat opening black sequin dance costume

River Deep Mountain High
Darlene – repeat opening teal beaded costume

Female Back-up Singers
1. Repeat black sequins
3. Repeat black sequins
4. Repeat black sequins
5. Repeat black sequins
6. Repeat black sequins
7. Repeat black sequins

Male Back-up Singers
1. Repeat black sequins
3. Repeat black sequins
4. Repeat black sequins
5. Repeat black sequins
6. Repeat black sequins

Finale – We're Gonna Make It After All
Producer – black pants, turquoise shirt, black & silver studded leather tunic, black shoes
Jeff – brown silk pants, brown silk shirt, brown shoes, bronze and gold beaded vest
Annie – black unitard, purple silk blouse, black & silver tunic, black boots
Ellie – repeat pink & black sequins
Darlene – repeat teal beaded costume
Young Ellie – yellow sequinned sheath shirtwaist dress, beige shoes

Female Back-up Singers
1. Repeat black sequins
2. Repeat black sequins
3. Repeat black sequins
4. Repeat black sequins
5. Repeat black sequins
6. Repeat black sequins
7. Repeat black sequins

Male Back-up Singers
1. Repeat black sequins
2. Repeat black sequins
3. Repeat black sequins
4. Repeat black sequins
5. Repeat black sequins
6. Repeat black sequins

PROPS

upright piano		onstage, under yellow platter

BE MY BABY

3 beehives	Annie, Barbara, Pattie	right

Levittown

accordion (also used later in *BOMP SHU BOM* and *WE'RE GONNA MAKE IT*)	Ellie	always works from stage left
pin cushion with pins on wrist band	Rosie	personal

Writers' Crossover

dark glasses (also used in later scenes)	Jeff	personal
	Keith	personal
	Peter	personal
	Lon	personal
	Joey	personal
sheet of music	Jeff	right

Brill Building

sheet of music	Ellie	left
dark glasses (also used in later scenes)	Gus	personal
candy bar	Gus	personal

I WANNA LOVE HIM

candy bar (double)	Gus	personal

AND THEN HE KISSED ME

lips	carried on by Gina & Lon	left

Lovers' Lane

2 cars	Danny	left
	Keith	left
1 car	Joey	right
pad & pencil	Jeff	left

Brill Building (Marriage Proposal)

piano stool	set by props crew during *Lovers' Lane*	left
pen on cord worn around neck	Ellie	left

CHAPEL OF LOVE

bridal bouquet	Eflhe	right
bridesmaids' bouquets	Jodi	left
	Barbara	left
	Jasmine	left
	Shirley	left

Medley

2 practical stand mikes	Chris	right
	Peter	left

Motorcycle Scene

sheet of music	Ellie	left
check	Jeff	left
canvas luggage	Gus	left
several pieces of music	Gus	left

LEADER OF THE PACK

5 motorcycle handlebars	Keith	up center
	Danny	up center
	Joey	up center
	Chris	up center
	Lon	up center
5 eyeglasses with lights	Keith	up center
	Danny	up center
	Joey	up center
	Chris	up center
	Lon	up center
4 eyeglasses with lights	Barbara	left
	Jasmine	left
	Jodi	left
	Shirley	left

(At the end of LEADER OF THE PACK, sheet music and the stool are struck by the props crew to offstage left.)

Dressing Scene

purse with makeup	Ellie	right

Chez Smooch

BMI awards	Ellie	right

	Gus	right
dark glasses	Ellie	right
Waitress pad and pencil	Waitress	right
flash camera	Waitress	right
lips settee	set by props crew	right
	Christmas Card Scene	
Christmas cards	Ellie	right
Reunion Scene		
coffee mug	Gus	right
headsets	Gus	right
	Jeff	right
	I CAN HEAR MUSIC	
practical mike stand (double)	Keith	right

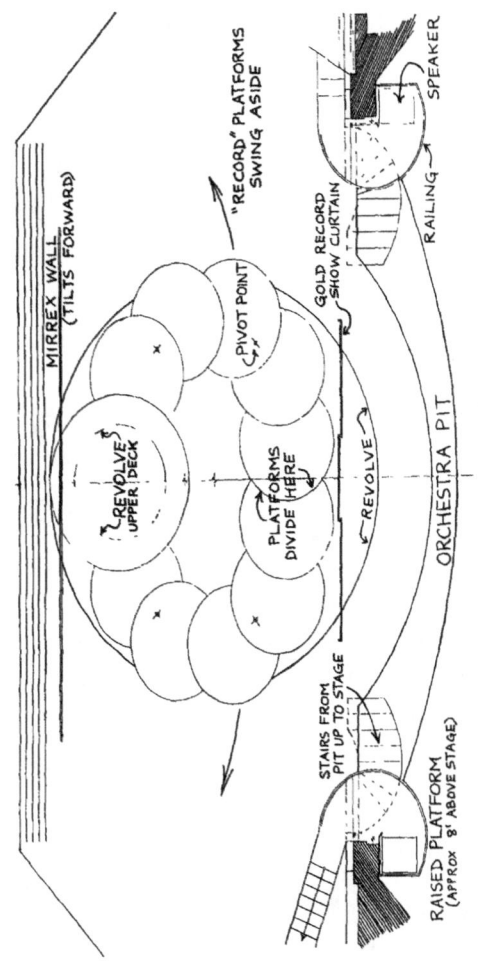

MIRREX WALL (TILTS FORWARD)

"RECORD" PLATFORMS SWING ASIDE

PIVOT POINT

REVOLVE UPPER DECK

PLATFORMS DIVIDE HERE

GOLD RECORD SHOW CURTAIN

REVOLVE

SPEAKER

RAILING

ORCHESTRA PIT

STAIRS FROM PIT UP TO STAGE

RAISED PLATFORM (APPROX 8' ABOVE STAGE)

SCENE DESIGN: LEADER OF THE PACK